TRIGGER DANCE

OTHER BOOKS BY DIANE GLANCY:

One Age in a Dream (Milkweed Editions, 1986)

Offering (Holy Cow! Press, 1988)

Iron Woman (New Rivers Press, 1990)

Lone Dog's Winter Count (West End Press, 1991)

TRIGGER
D A N C E

by
Diane Glancy

FICTION COLLECTIVE TWO
BOULDER • NORMAL • BROOKLYN

This book is the winner of the 1990 Charles H. and N. Mildred
Nilon Excellence in Minority Fiction Award, sponsored by the
University of Colorado and Fiction Collective Two.

Published jointly by the University of Colorado at Boulder,
and Fiction Collective Two, with assistance from the National
Endowment for the Arts; the support of the Publications
Center, University of Colorado at Boulder; and the cooperation
of Brooklyn College, Illinois State University, Normal, and
Teachers & Writers Collaborative.

Forward all inquiries to: Fiction Collective Two, English
Department Publications Center, University of Colorado at
Boulder, Boulder, CO 80309-0494.

Library of Congress Cataloging in Publication Data

90-071040
Glancy, Diane.
    Trigger Dance
I. Title

ISBN: 0-932511-35-x
ISBN: 0-932511-36-8 (pbk.)

Distributed by The Talman Company

Acknowledgements

The Alaska Quarterly for "Holation"; *Blue Pitcher* for "Anadarko Pow Wow"; *Midland Review* for "Yote U Ey"; *Anemone* for "Trying on the Hat"; *Oxford Magazine* for "In This Mission School"; *Born at the Crossroads: Voices of Mixed Heritage Women* for "Aunt Parnetta's Electric Blisters"; *Sing Heavenly Muse!* for second prize and publication of "The Voluble Rap" in their Midwestern Women of Color issue; *Whispering Wind Magazine* for "Sweat Lodge", which appears as part of "Trigger Dance"; *Gettysburg Review* for "Broken Spell"; *Contemporary Native American Fiction* for "Aunt Parnetta's Electric Blisters."

I thank *Toyon Magazine*, Humboldt State University, for their award of finalist to "Regretfully."

I thank the Oklahoma Federation of Writers for their awards to "The Orchard" and "Keyo."

I also thank the Tulsa Library for their awards to "A Sense of Continuity and Presence" and "Aunt Parnetta's Electric Blisters."

This is not so much for a people
as it is a place—
Oklahoma
Where I first heard
the voices of my heritage.

TRIGGER DANCE

Anadarko Pow Wow

WHAY NAH. THE OLD LANGUAGE LODGED IN THEIR HEAD. FOR this, then, the young men danced. Kiowa, Caddo, Creek, Chickasaw, Cheyenne, Ponca, Pawnee, Osage, Cherokee.

For this, they danced in headdress & feather bustle, bells & leggings, beaded moccasins & breastplate. Not all of them, no, not the boys walking the fairgrounds snagging girls. They had already dropped into hopelessness. For them, the sun rolled across the plains & off the edge of Oklahoma like a gutter ball.

But the young men in the bright arena danced the buffalo dance, snake dance, straightdance, the fancy war dance, while singers chanted "hey ye hey ye" & beat their drums in the heat.

They danced on the trail up through the black sky where ancestors waited with the bruised face of the moon. Even if their lives were a hole they crawled into, they danced on the great plains of the country with a flag with red stripes of blood.

A pah nuh. They heard the dead language again.

Pin-cushion, all of them.

How had they survived their struggle & defeat? Why hadn't their race folded up & disappeared in the dust where the feet of the young men beat the arena ground?

Nuh hekka.

The warrior moon steadied the dusty haze of the fairgrounds where a stream of cars still drove into the field to park.

Meanwhile the young men strutted in the arena like prairie cocks, looking here, looking there, in step with the drums as though strange ballet dancers or tiptoeing bowlers, vibrant, transcending, in tune with the dead.

Aunt Parnetta's Electric Blisters

Some stories can be told only in the winter.
This is not one of them
because the fridge is for Parnetta
where it's always winter.

1.

HEY CHEKTA! ALL THIS AND NOW THE REFRIGERATOR BROKE. Uncle Filo scratched the long gray hairs that hung in a tattered braid on his back. All that foot stomping and fancy dancing. Old warriors still at it. But when did it help? Aunt Parnetta asked. The fridge ran all through the cold winter when she could have set the milk and eggs in the snow. The fish and meat from the last hunt. The fridge had walked through the spring when she had her quilt and beading money. Now her penny jar was empty and it was hot and the glossy white box broke. The coffin! If grandpa died, they could put him in it with his war ax and tomahawk. His old dog even. But how would she get a new fridge?

The repairman said he couldn't repair it. Whee choo tun. Filo loaded his shotgun and sent a bullet right through it. Well, he said, a man had to take revenge. Had to stand against civilization. He watched the summer sky for change as though the stars were white leaves across the hill. Would the stars fall? Would Filo have to rake them when cool weather came again? Filo coughed and scratched his shirt pocket as though something crawled deep within his breastbone. His heart maybe, if he ever found it.

Aunt Parnetta stood at the sink, soaking the sheets before she washed them.

"Dern't nothin' we dud ever werk?" Parnetta asked, poling the sheets with her stick.

"We bought that ferge back twenty yars," Filo told her. "And it nerked since then."

"Weld, derned," she answered. "Could have goned longer til the frost cobered us. Culb ha' set the milk ertside. But nowd. It weren't werk that far."

"Nope," Filo commented. "It weren't."

Parnetta looked at her beadwork. Her hands flopped at her sides. She couldn't have it done for a long time. She looked at the white patent-leathery box. Big enough for the both of them. For the cow if it died.

"Set it out in the backyard with the last one we had."

They drove to Tahlequah that afternoon, Filo's truck squirting dust and pinging rocks.

They parked in front of the hardware store on Muskogee Street. The regiments of stoves, fridges, washers, dryers, stood like white soldiers. The Yellow Hair Custer was there to command them. Little Big Horn. Whu chutah! The prices! Three hundred crackers.

"Some mord than thad," Filo surmised, his flannel shirt-collar tucked under itself, his braid sideways like a rattler on his back.

"Filo, I dern't think we shulb decide terday."

"No," the immediate answer stummed from his mouth like a roach from under the baseboard in the kitchen.

"We're just lookin'."

"Of course," said Custer.

They walked to the door leaving the stoves, washers, dryers, the televisions all blaring together, and the fridges lined up for battle.

Filo lifted his hand from the rattled truck.

"Surrender," Parnetta said. "Izend thad the way id always iz?"

The truck spurted and spattered and shook Filo and Aunt Parnetta before Filo got it backed into the street. The forward gear didn't buck as much as the backward.

When they got home, Filo took the back off the fridge and looked at the motor. It could move a load of hay up the road if it had wheels. Could freeze half the fish in the pond. The minute coils, the twisting intestines of the fridge like the hog he butchered last winter, also with a bullet hole in its head.

"Nothin' we dude nerks." Parnetta watched him from the kitchen window. "Everythin' against uz," she grumbled to herself.

Filo got his war feather from the shed, put it in his crooked braid. He stomped his feet, hooted. Filo, the medicine man, transcended to the spirit world for the refrigerator. He shook each kink and bolt. The spirit of cold itself. He whooped and warred in the yard for nearly half an hour.

"Not with a bullet hole in it," Parnetta shook her head and wiped the sweat from her face.

He got his wrench and hack saw, the axe and hammer. It was dead now for sure. Parnetta knew it at the sink. It was the thing that would be buried in the backyard. "Like most of us libed," Aunt Parnetta talked to herself. "Filled with our own workings, not doint what we shulb."

Parnetta hung the sheets in the yard, white and square as the fridge itself.

2.

The new refrigerator came in a delivery truck. It stood in the kitchen. Bought on time at a bargain. Cheapest in the store. Filo made sure of it. The interest over five years would be as much as the fridge. Aunt Parnetta tried to explain it to him. The men set the fridge where Parnetta instructed them. They adjusted and leveled the little hog feet. They gave Parnetta the packet of information, the guarantee. Then drove off in victory. The new smell of the gleaming white inside as though cleansed by cedar from the Keetowah fire.

Aunt Parnetta had Filo take her to the grocery store on the old road to Tahlequah. She loaded the cart with milk and butter. Frozen waffles. Orange juice. Anything that had to be kept cool. The fridge made noise, she thought, she would get used to it. But in the night, she heard the fridge. It seemed to fill her dreams. She had trouble going to sleep, even on the clean white sheets, and she had trouble staying asleep. The fridge was like a giant hog in the kitchen. Rutting and snorting all night. She got up once and unplugged it. Waking early the next morning to plug it in again before the milk and eggs got warm.

"That ferge bother yeu, Filo?" she asked.

"Nord."

Aunt Parnetta peeled her potatoes outside. She mended Filo's shirts under the shade tree. She didn't soak anything in the kitchen sink anymore, not even the sheets or Filo's socks. There just were things she had to endure, she grumped. That's the way it was.

When the grandchildren visited, she had them run in the kitchen for whatever she needed. They picnicked on the old watermelon table in the backyard. She put up the old teepee for them to sleep in.

"Late in the summer fer that?" Filo quizzed her.

"Nert. It waz nert to get homesick for the summer that's leabing us like the childurn." She gratified him with her keen sense. Parnetta could think up anything for what she wanted to do.

Several nights Filo returned to their bed with its geese-in-flight-over-the-swamp pattern quilt, but Aunt Parnetta stayed in the teepee under the stars.

"We bined muried thurdy yars. Git in the house," Filo said one night under the white leaves of the stars.

"I can't sleep cause of that wild hog in the kitchen," Aunt Parnetta said. "I tald yeu that."

"Hey chekta!" Filo answered her. "Why didn't yeu teld me so I knowd whad yeu said." Filo covered the white box of the fridge with the geese quilt and an old Indian blanket he got from the shed. "Werd yeu stayed out thar all winder?"

"Til the beast we got in thar dies."

"Hawly gizard," Filo spurted. "Thard be anuther twendy yars!"

Aunt Parnetta was comforted by the bedroom that night. Old Filo's snore after he made his snorting love to her. The gray and blue striped wallpaper with its watermarks. The stove pipe curling up to the wall like a hog tail. The bureau dresser with a little doily and her hairbrush. Pictures by their grandchildren. A turquoise coyote and a ghostly figure the boy told her was Running Wind.

She fell into a light sleep where the white stars blew down from the sky, flapping like the white sheets on the line. She nudged Filo to get his rake. He turned sharply against her. Parnetta woke and sat on the edge of the bed.

"Yeu wand me to cuber the furge wid something else?" Filo asked from his sleep.

"No," Aunt Parnetta answered him. "Nod unless id be the polar ice cap."

3.

Now it was an old trip to Minnesota when she was a girl. Parnetta saw herself in a plaid shirt and braids. Had her hair been that dark? Now it was streaked with gray. Everything was like a child's drawing. Exaggerated. The way dreams were sometimes. A sun in the left corner of the picture. The trail of chimney smoke from the narrow house. It was cold. So cold that everything creaked. She heard cars running late into the night. Early mornings, steam growled out of the exhaust. The pane of window-glass in the front door had been somewhere else. Old lettering showed up in the frost. Bones remembered their aches in the cold. Teeth, their hurt. The way Parnetta remembered every bad thing that happened. She dwelled on it.

The cold place was shriveled to the small upright rectangle in her chest, holding the fish her grandson caught in the river. That's where the cold place was. Right inside her heart. No longer pumping like the blinker lights she saw in town. She was the Minnesota winter she remembered as a child. The electricity it took to keep her cold! The energy. The moon over her like a ceiling light. Stars were holes where the rain came in. The dripping buckets. All of them like Parnetta. The hurrrrrrrrrr of the fridge. Off. On. All night. That white box. Wild boar! Think of it. She didn't always know why she was disgruntled. She just was. She saw herself as the fridge. A frozen fish stiff as a brick. The Great Spirit had her pegged. Could she find her heart, maybe, if she looked somewhere in her chest?

Hurrrrrrrr. Rat-tat-at-rat. Hurrr. The fridge came on again, and startled, she woke and teetered slightly on the edge of the bed while it growled.

But she was a stranger in this world. An Indian in a white man's land. "Even the furge's whate," Parnetta told the Great Spirit.

"Wasn't everybody a stranger and pilgrim?" The Great Spirit seemed to speak to her, or it was her own thoughts wandering in her head.

"No," Parnetta insisted. Some people were at home on this earth, moving with ease. She would ask the Great Spirit more about it later. When he finally yanked the life out of her like the pin in a grenade.

Suddenly Parnetta realized that she was always moaning like the fridge. Maybe she irritated the Great Spirit like the white box irritated her. Did she sound that way to anyone else? Was that the Spirit's revenge? She was stuck with the cheapest box in the store. In fact, in her fears, wasn't it a white boar that would tear into the room and eat her soon as she got good and asleep?

Hadn't she seen the worst in things? Didn't she weigh herself in the winter with her coat on? Sometimes wrapped in the blanket also?

"Filo?" She turned to him. But he was out cold. Farther away than Minnesota.

"No. Just think about it, Parnetta," her thoughts seemed to say. The Spirit had blessed her life. But inside the white refrigerator of herself—inside the coils, an ice river surged. A glacier mowed its way across a continent. Everything frozen for eons. In need of a Keetowah fire. Heat. The warmth of the Great Spirit. Filo was only a spark. He could not warm her. Even though he tried.

Maybe the Great Spirit had done her a favor. Hope like white sparks of stars glistened in her head. The electric blisters. TEMPORARY! She could shut up. She belonged to the Spirit. He had just unplugged her a minute. Took his shotgun right through her head.

The leaves growled and spewed white sparks in the sky. It was a volcano from the moon. Erupting in the heavens. Sending down its white sparklers like the pinwheels Filo used to nail on trees. It was the bright sparks of the Keetowah fire, the holy bonfire from which smaller fires burned, spreading the purification of the Great Spirit into each house. Into each hard, old pinecone heart.

Keyo

THE JULY SUN FLATTENED THE PRAIRIE TO A TABLE WHERE KEYO
sat in the school house when he was in trouble. He was the
oldest in class and still couldn't read. The words moved
under his eyes and nothing happened. They might as well
be bats or ghosts that swooped over the cabin at night. He
was never sure.

The teacher looked from the window again. She sighed
and wiped her forehead with a handkerchief. She showed
him the consonants. This week it was *r*. He had to read the
words that started with *r* and listen to the first sound in
each word. *Red, rabbit, reason, READ!* Then the teacher
gave him syllables. *Ble*, *dle*, *ple*, *gle*. After that he had to
read a paragraph and answer her questions. But he never
knew what the answers were because he couldn't read the
paragraph.

The teacher showed him his vocabulary words for the
next week. They were black spots on the page with the

power of buckshot. Stronger than he was. How he wished he were in his brothers' truck. If only they could get it started, they would ride to Chickasha, Oklahoma, and get drunk for the night. When the woman got up and left the room, Keyo closed the book.

The whole earth roasted. The red soil plowed up for corn, it shuddered in fields, clapping its stupid hands. The sun always ran out of the southwest, across the plains, never stopping, like wind, like the white man. No, Indians were behind the margin of the paper. All the words moved on the page, flicked under his eyes. They were the far away city and he was outside. His brothers had gone and come back. No matter how many winters and summers Keyo spent in school, he knew he wouldn't make it either.

Outside the window, he saw a corncrib on stilts, fields changing every day with heat, the glare of sky. How could he sit in class all his life and not know anything? How could the words, small rodents that they were, run away from him and burrow into the page? Sometimes he saw nothing but a dull glare from the book.

Keyo had to stay at the table because he punched a boy who insulted him—called him a stupid slug. A slow slug. Did it matter? Keyo's body filled with power that could ride a horse across the prairie, or endure the vision quest. Keyo had to hit. It was the only thing he could do—he let his anger fly like an arrow into a buffalo. Now the kid was in the clinic with a broken face.

Perhaps if words were rabbits running in the field, he could aim his rifle and plug them. Could he think of them in that way and learn to read? No—he looked at the girls as they walked by the window. Their screams on the play-

ground after school sounded like a litter of new animals.
Their bodies already fuzzy in places? Their soft hair made
Keyo think of other things than the trouble he was in. Not
words, no. He didn't think in them. But pictures went
through Keyo's mind. For now, he had to sit at the table
until they decided what to do with him. He made the school
look bad. Its programs and teaching didn't affect him. He
should be out in the field working in the corn, or weeding
the garden for his mother, or finding his father asleep in
some back alley in Calumet.

Nothing worked. He would not learn to read. The kids
would laugh again. Kids smaller than him. Words were
easy for them. They opened a book and knew what it said.
They even made stories about Indians. Wasn't there some
on the wall of the school room? How could they write about
his life? Because of their WORDS. Those horrible black
things like fleas. Worse! TICKS that hid under the skin
down in the fur of Roofer, his dog. He had picked them out
of his own leg too with the hot head of a match. The pain was
the same he felt trying to read. What was the matter with
him?

He remembered his little sister at her Easy-Bake Oven,
reading her mother's recipes. Red beans. Fry bread. She
pointed her finger to the words for Keyo. Repeated the
words patiently for him. He remembered the part about the
fried rabbit and squirrel. Disjoint the legs, split down the
back. Soak in salted water. Brown in hot fat. If the animal
was of an uncertain age, they had to add a small bit of hot
water. Keyo's sister had watched his mouth as he tried to
read the words she pointed to. His stomach ached for the
breads and meats she had read, but he couldn't say the

words without her repeating them several times. And never by himself the first time. He sat at the table in the school house in his combat tennis shoes, camouflage pants, and red kerchief for an arm band.

He looked from the window. Already the ruin of the moon up over the prairie. Pale, ghostly, and crumbled. Or else it was dressed in its spotted pajamas. Fat as his mother with another baby.

Keyo was angry she would bring someone else in the world like him. He wiped his sweat. If the baby were like his sister, that would be all right. But not another one like him. He was angry he was born in a world that required books. He was angry at words that swarmed like insects in the creek bottoms, forever out of reach, forever spelling their own secret language that left him a stranger in their world.

Trying on the Hat

IN MY MOTHER-IN-LAW'S HOUSE, AT THE FRONT HALL CLOSET
where wood planks run under the door, I turn the old brass
knob that must be a buffalo-eye watching the prairie.

Hey nuh nuh.

Inside: old coats she hasn't worn since her husband was
alive; garment bag where an evening dress still twirls from
the last time she danced in his arms. And there, on a shelf
above the clothes pole: hat boxes—I pull them down and
something spills to the ground like tiny flower seeds from
the corner of a packet.

I find a brown velvet hat with veil and feather and put
it on my head: another rush of the fine particles like dirt
that children throw at one another in dust fights—Oh, she
says, those are cockroach eggs. I haven't been in that closet
for years.

I take the hat from my head, brush through my hair
with my hands. I hear them hit the floor like grease from
a sizzling pot. Hisstpos.

When I shake the hat, a puff-cloud rises from the soft and disintegrating velvet where cockroaches breed under buffalo skin and a rotting head with the brass eye that still turns in its socket.

But among these clothes, I think how they got through depression and war and the giddy years that followed, and I think there must be a way for us too—my sick husband and I—he in his old room talking to himself—me looking for something to do to take my mind off—and the children wrapped like anvils in their blankets when we come for a weekend to hide.

Their sweet heads asleep while mine turns angrily to their father for his neglect of us, his drinking and torment. And all these minute seeds that tumble out of brown velvet could have been shiny seeds that would be four o'clocks in spring soil.

In these clothes my mother-in-law wore, some of them from when she was younger than me, I think somehow we endure like these coats and evening dresses while cockroaches nurse our oozing wounds and we wake burning in the night.

The pressure runs over us with these beasts, their two antennae raised like swords, their legs running on chaintracks of tanks the children drive fighting off the enemy with their little bows and arrows.

Hey chu nu ney.

I sat in your closet as a child, Great Buffalo, when my parents were on a rampage and dust from the stampede robbed me of breath. I stuck my fingers in my ears, put a kerchief on my nose until hooves and wagon wheels passed. No nuh. I am in your closet again—

The smell of sweet cedar, Jesus of Lebanon, Christ of prunes and peace with hands upheld and the cannon fire against me fails.

The closet pole: a tightrope between the walls, and I have to walk it, carrying children into the house, my head enormous with desperation.

The far, far fall I would take but the thin closet pole, the tightrope wire, is a highway—oh, think of it as a slab of concrete in space from which there is no fall.

I walk solidly with joyous feet, Great Buffalo, in your dank skull, your brass eye watches.

Fry bread splatters and a mother-in-law hisses about her velvet hat, while I enter the dark insides of my head, my own swords raised, planting seeds from packets of flowers that would bloom.

Broken Spell

TREES LEANED TOWARD THE SIDEWALK LIKE A HAND SHOVED them down. The wind stampeded across the road. Then rain rushed at an angle past the window under angry bites of lightning.

"Cay mah nok tah." Anna America sat in her chair. Her flowered cotton robe was stiff. She'd sweated during her nap that afternoon, then dried. "Maybe this will break the hot spell." Anna held her cane on her lap. Her head rested against the back of the tall chair, two fingers across her mouth. The rain coughed over the roof, splattered on the ground in puddles.

"Into the nineties & it's only turned June," she summed. "The summer'll be in the hundreds before it gets started."

But this storm would cut into the heat. For a while, anyway, Northeastern Oklahoma Cherokee County Shelter would be cooler. Anna America could doze & remember when she'd been in school long ago. She could remember her woven shawls, seed-bowls, the moon as heavy as a horse blanket. She could think of nights the heat held on like children clawing at their mothers when they came to the shelter. She tried to turn away its smell, the eyes in the chairs out in the hall, disappearing into wrinkles, some of them crying out.

"Push me that stool. I need to get this old stump up off the ground." Anna made her arm fly. Bird with five wings.

"You got your sash wrapped around your foot," an old woman said at the door. "Don't fall when you get up."

"I got nowhere to go."

The rain made nasty splats on the steps. Anna remembered the angry nurse when the old women made puddles. She must have dozed again. For a moment she was in her house with its bed & chest of drawers, the table & one chair. She chopped the other chairs for firewood late last winter. She startled herself awake with the memory of her son, William America, carrying her out of her house like a bride. Surely the veil of death on her. She'd never go back. Why couldn't she die?

A light bulb flickered in the hall. The thoughts in her head drove her farther into memory. Her daughter & two of her sons in alcoholic stupors. She had been there herself several times before she got ahold of the cross. Drinking her way across the country. She had years she couldn't remember. Her head fell forward a moment in her chair. She slept off & on all day, then spent hours awake in the night, angered that she couldn't sleep. Doting on war chants. Buckaroo Braves. Indians in rodeos. The nurse came in & hushed her, tied her to her chair as though the hand of the storm pushed her down too. The nurse said she would stuff a sock in Anna's mouth if she didn't shut up.

Her head felt like a hundred pounds & hurt the back of her neck. She rallied. "Heck chaw nah maw."

"You can't scream in the middle of the night. There're some who sleep." The nurse was always grouchy.

"I can't sleep!" Anna shouted at her with a gritty voice. "The storm!"

If only she didn't doze all day. But what else was there to do? When she slept, little children came into her dreams. She imagined she was on the prairie again running to the mission school, riding her pony later to the consolidated school, baking bread & cakes with her mother. Loving her husband until he got so drunk she couldn't tolerate his presence. Then she'd wake a moment. The Shelter for Aged Indians was better than the memory of him.

It seemed the animals growled sometimes at night, especially when she was back in her house with young children & her husband on the rampage. He'd stay out in the bushes raking the house, walking on the roof just to scare her & the children. Sometimes she still saw the red eyes, the electrical cord going up to the moon. On clear nights its milky light shone through the curtains at the window. Her chants cracked under her old voice. She could not hold them back. The nurse tied a rag around Anna's face, covering her mouth. She hummed the tune that rose from her heart. Visions the old Indians had were usually calm affairs. No one could raise their voices, but croaked like toads that came out after rain.

The warning siren eeked from the corner of the greenish sky, slobbered over the edge of Cherokee County, then shut off. Wind storms came all the time. Anna was not interested in them. She was tied to her chair. Maybe she would fly with the roof to the edge of town, if all the noise was about a tornado. Maybe she would drown in a downpour if all they were getting was rain. Then her life would end in water as it had begun in the womb. Yes, she had liked that lesson in school.

Her skin felt puckered & thin. Would the Great Spirit recognize her as the creature he had once made? Didn't the minister say that God looked on the heart & not the outward part? In the light that came in the door from the hall, she could see the snarl of veins just under the surface. Her joints were swollen, aching. Her head forgetful, cranky, afraid.

In the old days the fathers died easily. Now everything seemed out of whack. Maybe the whites mutated death also, once quick & glorious, easy as corn bread. Now it contorted before her in screams, cries, agonies she heard all around her, even sometimes she guessed from her own mouth. A prolonging of it all. How many had she sat with? Grandmothers who went on to the hunting grounds, humming in joy to rise from the earth. Her thumb twitched against her side & woke her a moment. She thought someone touched her, shoved her slightly like the trees calmer now after their tremors. Had the storm already passed? Had they left her in her chair all night or had she been in bed & forgotten? Maybe the storm came in the early evening & they had not put her to bed yet. Maybe they'd simply forgotten her on their rounds.

Anna thought often of her children. How she'd put them in bureau drawers to sleep when they were babies because there was no place else for them. How she'd been stupid

with drink, sometimes probably falling asleep as she fed
them & they must have crawled & wandered around the
house picking up crumbs to eat, crying, their noses always
running. Maybe they had bumped against her until they
woke her & she, sick with drink, probably whacked them in
the head to shut their mouths. They had learned silence &
pain. Had always known it. How had it fallen apart? How
had they survived? She remembered the mission school
when William & the other children painted wigwams &
teepees & wore tribal costume & sang as their fathers &
grandfathers had. & she, drying out, watched them until
years later, her heart grew warm & she heard the prayer-
hum within herself. She sang it again, even though the rag
was around her face. What fluttered then in her chest? The
Great Spirit offered forgiveness & new life. She knew that
if she knew nothing else on this flat earth.

Yes, the rain had already slackened, sputtered off
toward the east. "Let them have it," she said. What day was
it? What month? She couldn't think anymore. It all shat-
tered before her. Who cared what time it was anyway? Did
her grandfathers have clocks?

Let the heat flush out everyone's bad temper. She was
through with the earth. The treacherous place. Electric
horse-blanket for a moon. What a waste it had been. Her
husband no longer on her. No, Anna had not remembered
that in a long time. She felt a flush for a moment between
her legs as she thought of him. Why did it come back in her
old age? She touched herself in her robe, then took her hand
away. The nurse would tie her hands to the sides of her
chair if she saw her. His love had turned yellow as whiskey
anyway & the pleasure he gave her didn't last.

The siren retched with spasm again. She heard a roar pass over. Maybe she would rise into the storm & pass out of this civilization. She'd never been part of it anyway. She would be glad to leave the lumps of her legs in their purple houseshoes with blue veins popping out everywhere. She felt her sagging breasts, the wrinkled skin inside the flowered robe. Even her mind played tricks. The trickster, coyote.

She woke up young again until she looked down at her arms & saw the robe fallen open while a woman washed her, folds of skin on her narrow belly. Was it morning? Where was the storm gone?

"Come on, Anna America," the gross nurse said. "You can wail all night, but in the morning, not half of you comes back."

Anna's robe was stained with food. Death was a kicker. The nurse talked about a limb from the tree across the porch. The storm was gone, but no, not the heat. She'd been wrong. The wind came back with the heat & tricked her.

The storm had come & gone & Anna had known little of it. She was taking care of the children, chasing off her husband, then another man had come, & she had to watch out for him too. She didn't want him on the place. A man was just another child to take care of. She threw rocks at him.

Anna couldn't remember the day if they told her a hundred times, pinned it to her nose. She didn't know her children sometimes when they came. She'd think of them playing in the mud by the house & they'd come in dirty & she'd tell them to wash, & it would be William America standing there saying it was her grandsons. She'd tell them to go away, but they screamed their names in her face so she could understand. Why didn't they shut up? No, she put her two fingers across her mouth. She wanted them to come.

Her head fell forward, lost somewhere in her thoughts. The red eye of the sky looked in the window, the land toward which she moved but which she couldn't get to for some reason. She always felt held back. That hand again.

Life was enough to kill hundreds & thousands of buffalo. It could put Indians in jets & real estate. Bombs away. Now death was another life in itself. "He sheck aa." Anna choked out her prayer-language.

She had begun life as a polliwog in the womb. She remembered the lesson in school again before she had quit. Then she turned animal, breathed the air of this world. She had gone through every stage but the wings. Maybe they weren't left out after all. No, the Great Spirit knew what he was doing. She had borne the wings in her spirit all her life. She remembered now they had carried her along. That's what she had felt in her chest. The wings were coming to her now in death. Maybe they were already on her back. Wouldn't she love for the gross nurse to find them. Anna tried to feel her back, but couldn't reach it. One day soon she would walk to the sky. Yes, she nodded to herself. She would pull the blanket moon over her, nothing behind her but a moan or a whimper.

A Sense of Continuity
and Presence

CARS LINED THE DRIVE ALONG THE OLD ROAD LIKE THEY DID
when Harrison was alive and Elma made a dinner that
everyone came for, not just to sit at the table and talk
politely, then leave, having one's family obligation over
with as they did at other houses, but Elma made the meal,
was the meal herself, talking and laughing at her end of the
table while Harrison, when he was alive, snorted and put
away enough to last several days.

"That's probably what killed him," Fillmore Running
Bear, his brother said, eyeing Elma for himself. "Heyye!
What an Indian he was." But Fillmore still had a wife, quiet
and regressing slowly into the grip of docility that always
threatened her and kept her from entering into a union like
Elma and Harrison had, or a union Fillmore assumed they
had from what he saw, but didn't know firsthand. And the
children came willingly and often, not to get anything, but
to be there with them. How did they do it? How did she do

it now that Harrison was gone? Fillmore's children ignored them or came out of duty when their mother with her measly and peeling words made them feel guilty, and they knew they had to come or be removed from that part of the tribe that was decent folks, which standard had been instilled in them.

Cars never lined the drive of the other Running Bear house: Fillmore's and his wife's. Their three children were wooden, not lively like Elma's and Harrison's. Why was he still alive, and not Harrison?

"It's hard to understand all right," Harrison's oldest son said to Fillmore, his uncle.

"I know, Bill," Fillmore patted his back as they seated themselves at the dinner table, and Fillmore watched Elma in the large square kitchen of her house where they had come for some occasion. Did it matter? They didn't have to have a reason to come for one of Elma's meals. It was a pleasure for them to get together at her house—the house that Harrison and Fillmore and some of the men from the tribe had built room by room. It even seemed as though Harrison were still among them. Fillmore took his eyes off Elma as she came to the table.

There was some disagreement between Harrison's daughters. One snapped at the other as they sat down. Fillmore asked the blessing on Elma's meal as Harrison had done. They fought just as much as Fillmore's children. He also had heard fierce words from his nephews, and in front of Elma too. But they recovered, laughed together again. Fillmore's children bore grudges; always had, bitter as gooseberries.

And now, at her end of the table, Fillmore thought Elma looked small. He remembered Harrison before his death when he lost weight and still wore the large suit of clothes that had once fit him. Harrison had been in his sixties when he died.

"Too early to call in the cows," Bill said.

"But he did, he did," Elma shrugged as though it was his will that he leave her alone with the years to watch the sunlight crawl down the pawpaws on the print wallpaper and remember him.

"Elm," Bill said to his mother. "You know the shed out back?"

"Of course." She nodded and passed the bowls.

"There's room enough to make it into sort of an apartment. Lots of folks live in smaller places than that, and pay a lot for it too."

"Which one of you is it that wants to come back?" She paused. Fillmore sat on the edge of his chair as he spooned her green beans on his plate. "Or is it for me?"

"No, Elm. We're not putting you out yet."

"Deen needs a place," Bill's wife stated.

"He's always coming back to us, can't make it on his own. We haven't got room," Bill started to eat.

"The shed isn't big enough for the two of them."

"There's only one of them now," Bill's wife said.

Elma was silent. The table seemed frozen for a moment. "He lives with a girl for several years, causing us grief," she said, "and leaves her after that?"

Deen swallowed with effort.

"She left him."

"So you are pushing the responsibility of your abandoned son off on me?" she asked Bill.

"That's right, Elm. Though I don't look at it exactly like that—you see, he can help—"

"I won't have him." Elma interrupted her son. "Let him go back and to the girl and straighten out whatever is wrong."

"He can't." Bill's wife passed the relish.

"I've tried, grandma," Deen said.

"She decided she didn't want to be married after all." Bill dropped the spoon in his saucer.

"Isn't that too bad," Elma said curtly. "So I get Beets because no one else wants him?" Elma said that without thinking. Deen's red cheeks flared, and with his dislike of that vegetable, his grandfather Harrison had given him that name.

"You get Deen because you can do something for him and he for you—"

"Will you pay me?"

"No, mother, I won't. But as I started to say—several times now—I'll wire the shed and insulate the walls, install plumbing. It will raise the value of your property."

"That might attract another man for you." It was Deen's turn to speak without thinking. Bill's wife stared at her son.

Elma laughed. "What would I do with another man who wasn't your grandfather?"

Fillmore pulled in his wandering thoughts and gave attention to the conversation, while his wife, who never had made contact with herself, was left in the field.

"I could help you keep the back lot mowed," Deen said.

"Yes, you could," she said. "Whether you live here or not."

"Do you know, mother"—Bill always called her mother and not Elm when he wanted something—"you could even paper it the way you want."

"That's generous of you," Elma told him. "I could buy and sell my house and yours if I wanted and don't you forget it. I have the stability of the years behind me and you are an unsettled lot."

"You couldn't buy my house, nor yours again, and don't you forget it, mother," Bill corrected her. "You are an aging woman with a small pension and if you weren't so conservative and grew your vegetables and canned and kept your savings, you would be looking for a shed to live in yourself."

One of Elma's daughters frowned at Bill as they ate.

"I won't tolerate divorce and you know it," Elma said, "when there's no real cause other than it just doesn't suit a person to be married, or because it's a strain." Bill's wife looked at the ceiling.

"It's not religion, but economics. That's what kept us all together in our day, and it's about to come to that again. Our Cherokee tribe was relocated in Indian Territory just over 150 years ago. We lived here on the margin of subsistence for several generations. We finally keep what we got a little of by holding onto it no matter what!"

The others looked at one another, then back to Elma, knowing what they were going to hear. The daughters and their families wanted to get up from the table, go into the other room and turn on television, but they knew Elma wouldn't hear of it. Deen could take the boys out in the backlot to play ball. But they would have to hear what Elma had to say.

"Families are too fragmented." They'd heard it all before. "One is here, one is there," she said, "no one can be tied down. That's why there was stability in our family. Harrison made the living. I stayed home and cooked meals, sewed, mended, beaded, washed. I made everyone else free to pursue their own course." Elma continued eating.

"But one has to be sacrificed for it. And it was you, the mother," Bill's wife protested.

"The elm tree," Bill said. "They knew what they were doing when they named you."

"Do I look like I have been sacrificed?" she asked him.

Fillmore was on the edge of his chair. By thunder, no! He thought. Elma's face was lit like the old barnyard lantern on the farm; the only light on the whole dark, vast place when he went out at night to make sure the door was fastened. And she was talking, lighting up the darkness that engulfed him most of the time, her meal in his stomach, her light on his face.

"That's the way it was when we were young." Elma gave Fillmore and the others a sense of presence, of continuity. Everything was all right because she was there.

It had always been that way. The years they built what they now had—the men working hard at their jobs during the day, and at night they would put up a few boards for another room on their houses as the wives had more children, and often Harrison or Fillmore would get discouraged because they felt they weren't getting anywhere and Elma would always be there with a warm meal, humming and saying to them that they were. And finally, they had gotten somewhere, Fillmore thought proudly to himself. Though there was still an outside staircase that climbed Elma's house. Harrison had planned a second story, but it had never come about.

Elma was transition from want to security, as her mother had been transition from the terrible dearth after the removal. She was transition from whatever was dark and uncertain and painful to whatever was light and comfort. And because of Elma, Fillmore would see them all someday, he knew as he listened to her, all the generations that would come after them and all the generations that went back in time, as Harrison had known when he listened to her, and was numbered now among, since his death, though at the last he was not wanting to go, depressed like he got before a trip.

"It wasn't that bad to be sacrificed," Elma said to Bill. "Do you remember Broken Arrow, where we used to go visit your father's sister after she moved?" Elma seemed to trail off on another thought.

"I couldn't forget with us fighting and Harrison cursing all the way and saying he'd never go again and us having to share a bed and hearing Harrison snore through the wall and thinking you must be part deaf, Elm, to have slept with him all those years." Bill stirred his coffee again.

"I got so tired of going there," one of Elma's daughter's fussed.

Fillmore thought of Harrison's snoring as they talked. Maybe even now the heavens sank and heaved with his breathing. It had the rhythm of the ancestral memories Elma carried: the movement of the tribe through the winter months of 1839 and 40 when their ancestors marched from Georgia to Oklahoma. Their groans and steady trudging were like house-noises that one gets used to. Fillmore wanted to dream the thoughts in his head, but at the same time he wanted to listen to Elma.

He was in her old house with rounded doorways and long halls and a breakfast nook in the kitchen that he had helped Harrison build for her. The big square kitchen was awkward, with everything away from everything else, and pots and pans hanging on the wall near the wire hen with excelsior and wooden eggs they used on the old farm, and outside, the stairway to the second floor which they had never finished—as though it went up to heaven—from which, Fillmore suddenly thought, Harrison could reach back down with his arm thin as a beet root and knock him in the head if he didn't stop thinking about Elma.

And she could make every day new though they had nothing new and had not really been anywhere but Broken Arrow to visit his sister after she married, and Fillmore had been in Elma's house 1000 times before that day and the same people were there with their grunting human natures and the same sofa and chairs and dining table were always before him in her house.

Even when Harrison was an old man holding rein on Elma because of his sickness, and he groaned with his fear of departing, she watched the light patterns on the wall and remembered old trips to Broken Arrow and the sun on the pawpaws curved into roads they had taken and she still could see the way.

They all listened to Elma then, her lively talk and laughter holding them, her words like buffalo that roamed the prairie.

Those that came after her in all their seeking of fulfillment would not know what Elma did in her sacrificing life.
She didn't have a job nor much time for herself as she saw
children go, and grandchildren come, and looked forward
to great-grandchildren with enlarged heads from all the
knowledge and fulfillment they would have in their own in-
dividual heads and would have to carry facts until they
looked like the old car Harrison had, and ate Volkswagen
soup, cooked with bark and tinder from linden groves and
would have forgotten in the mechanized heads that they
had once been a tribe of 17,000 Cherokees who crossed half
of this continent on foot in the dead of winter and survived
to build their lives again.

"AAmmmmmmmmmmm." Fillmore cleared his head.

"And grandchildren studying computers," Elma was
saying, "and not finding a place to live. I can understand
that. Harrison and I didn't have anything either for years.
But we stayed together and I won't hear of one divorce in
this family. All that wasted money. Put it into staying
together unless something is so terribly wrong that it can't
be overcome."

Deen tapped his foot impatiently on the floor.

"We're not all like you," one of the granddaughters said.

"Then bring in the dessert, if you can't do anything
else," she told them.

They got up gladly from the table.

"Character comes through grief and the grate of circum-
stance we can't get out of decently," she said. "Inner stuffing
doesn't come through seeking of self, but in the denying of
it. Then, and only then, something bigger than yourself
comes into your pandering heads."

"Yes, grandma," the girls said as they brought in Elma's corn pudding for dessert.

"Ammm," Fillmore said.

The days of Harrison's sickness peeled off like old skin in the reptile winter they had when he died, cold and indifferent to human need, giving Elma a reason to cry when everyone was gone, regretting she had lived, for the moment, to old age and the grandchildren growing into the computer age and living with girls who weren't their wives and change so vast she was swept under by it, but held on to what she knew and the way she knew to live and would not let them forget what it was like when one had the responsibility put upon them and stayed with it no matter how uncomfortable it grew at times. Her life probably seemed dull to Beets and the granddaughters, the niece and nephews and young in-laws in both Running Bear families. Nonetheless she would hold on to it so they would know how things had been, and probably still should be.

"It's all right, grandma," one of Bill's girls said. "I know what you're saying."

By thunder, Fillmore did too, and gave his wife an involuntary nudge of his leg in reflex to Elma's sermon, which held him captive, and nearly startled her out of her wits and she came alive, and looked at him shocked. A smile fluttered on her face in case something had been said she missed and should have reacted to. Fillmore wanted to nudge her again and wake her up and put into her the light Elma had. But he only confused her and made her seem more artificial in Elma's house, and it was why he came, why they came, not only for Elma's meal, for Deen was still having battle with the beets on his plate and raisins in his

bowl and the boys were restless after they finished their
corn pudding and needed, at last, to go outside, but it was
why they all came, to hear Elma spout like a buffalo stuck
in a mud wallow, and why cars lined up on the old road and
they always would come to Elma's house to see her on fire,

Yote U Ey

In the yard, shadows gather as I remove varnish from the table & chairs that were under the collapsed shed many winters, back in the corner where moonflower & night-shade root in dark earth.

Why did our father not tell us more? He, whose ancestors wrote their history on tipi hides, said nothing? We were Indian. That is all we should know? Now he is gone & the curse of silence is the paint & varnish I strip from the woodgrain in the table.

Brothers Ribbon visits on the old place as I scrape the loosened varnish. It is a brown stream of buffalo, the foam on the varnish like white birds that rode the backs of herds. It is as though we have no eyelids, I speak to Brothers of being Indian.

We pull boards from the rubble in the yard. I try to make a place of the old house, sweep out its floors, shake them in the yard, wash the tattered curtains, refinish the warped & peeling furniture from the shed.

I hear their moans from under the boards. I pull off my gloves, put my fingers in my ears. How long does their sound ooze from the ground?

Until we uncover them, Brothers Ribbon says.

Yote U Ey.

The varnish remover eats into my gloves, chews my fingers. I wash my hands.

You can never settle here, Brothers tells me.

The Ribbon is yours, I answer. Say what you must.

Leave the place.

No.

Why do you stay out here by yourself—sleeping on a cot by that broken window?

Because time pulls back— See: a woman enters the yard, pushing open the gate. She will not speak. She is our Indian grandmother, building a trellis by the shed that has since fallen. She can do anything, alone twenty years after her husband's death. She hears the voices of the yard. To her, the little wood slats on the picket fence are tongues. There, clematis took root with their need. How they clung.

Gardenia. White clematis. Flowers are still foreign to her. Maybe that is why she sat in the yard for hours watching their almost invisible entwining on the trellis. Finally she puts her finger into their tiny parts, tells them they are lovely. Their fragrant petals are the silky fur of a white beaver.

Eeot U Ey.

I would have escaped if I could. Maybe I would have been a white gardenia, my eyes waxy & thick-leafed.

Nothing would get through.

But we are born without eyelids. Everything is seen.

Now great-grandfather comes into the yard, who rode in the wagon around the town square dressed to kill, surrounded by eight children & his wife, fat as the Christmas goose. Sometimes he'd stand in the wagon, in his spats & coat, top hat, beads & feathers in his long braids, & ride proudly around the one block of the town. People at the dry goods & on the boardwalks of storefronts would call to him.

Why do we still see them? Brothers Ribbon pulls his headband over his eyes.

Because we have no eyelids, I tell him again. Besides, it is through them our curse comes. Our ancestors drifted while others persevered.

Great-grandfather killed a man, fled Indian Territory. We still suffer from his deed. Our broken hip & ribs, the despair of our minds, the inability to get anywhere.

Uote U Ey.

Great-grandfather sees our grandmother in the yard. It is when she falls & breaks her hip. He takes her into his arms again as though the wrinkled, gray-haired woman were his little daughter with a scraped knee. How they talk together without words.

See the scar on his hand, Brothers Ribbon points. A waterhole for our migration.

I am not going anywhere, I say. Here is the trellis in the rubble on which I climb. This yard stretched across us back to them. I scrape more of the festering varnish from the table, wash it with water from the well. The ground under the table looks like crumbs of pretzels covered with salt crystals. I lean on a corner of the table. The leg folds & it falls.

I take the apron off my black dress, go to get a hammer.

The old place is gone, Brothers Ribbon repeats.

But I will live on it, I say, even if I have to make a tipi from these trellis boards.

Then do one thing at a time, he instructs. Pick up the rubble or nail the table. Get something down before you go to another.

But I am staying, I say to him again for no reason. See, all our vehicles in the drive: your van & the old cars, wagons, horse & travaux. We are all here: our silent father \ grandmother \ great-grandfather \ our great-grandparents \ the ancestors.

They aren't really here—

They are, I answer. Some along the two gravel ruts to where a barn used to be in the backyard. We are a large family, I say & try to make the table leg straight again with nails, but it will not hold.

The table is warped, Brothers insists.

Then let's pull the boards off the rubble pile, one by one. Uncover their wailing. Let's DO SOMETHING!

Why don't you go into town, live in a house with gardenia trees in the yard that spread their white flowers over the streets. You could, Brothers says, you COULD! I think I am a tribal mourner, my eyes always swollen. I don't have room for lids. My nose runs. My ears open to the groans under the trellis. Those in town can stay there with their fragrance of magnolias.

Brothers pulls me to his van.

I do not like your friends, I say.

Come with me. They might help you with the place.

I ride down the road with Brothers Ribbon to get his friends. One brings a keg & Brothers says he doesn't like it. They'd better leave it alone until we get to my place. He won't get stopped again. Last time they hid out, just waiting, he says, to strip his van from him like a cocoon & leave him a coiled larva on the road.

Every night they go driving on the roads. Is there no end? an Indian says to me. I would answer, but he does not want one.

Brothers Ribbon swerves on the road.

Watch it, I say.

Leaves spill from the trees like copper pennies they throw in the bar in town. These fields clear as their whiskey. We drive before the hills under snow like humps of white ice cream.

Pin the tail on the donkey, one man takes another's ass.

Stop it! He says.

Get your hand off me—I say as they fool around.

Bejammers! The road veers as we wrestle in the van.

A swift knock in the head. A leg folds under the table & we fall. I hear silence. Then the moans of Brothers when he calls me.

I am here, I say. I see the hill rising from our heads. Our ancestors dance over us, a circle above our lidless eyes in the dark.

Yote E Uey.

Our great-grandparents did not think of the time ahead. None of them. The braves rode their horses. The squaws looked for berries.

They bundled up the tipi poles & packed the hides. The women tied travaux loaded with lodge pegs.

They wandered over the prairie.

Their dreams, a papoose-cradle-board when no child is born.

Hollow as baskets.

Still the women wove & braided ribbons & bands for the head & thighs of braves from a dead soldier's rifle.

In the bleak winter, visions thickened like ducks migrating north & night-watchers in the tribe saw stars dance with strings between them. The heavens painted braves before battle.

Even the women smelled stronger. The taste of their meager provisions sharpened. They held on to one another like school children on a walk.

Then somewhere in a black dawn, soldiers rushed into camp, clubbed with rifle butts, stabbed with bayonets. The Indians clawed back. They understood their vision of ripened cattails with the soft white fat of their innards POPPED over the land.

Afterwards, soldiers collected ear spools \ beaver ribs \ breech clout \ leggings \ moccasins \ parfleche \ fringed pipe bags from the dead.

At night, their feet cut loose from earth with a war-axe like prairie grass for sod houses.

Their tipis never again in fields of wahoo \ pawpaw \ black haw \ currant & chinquapin.

Slowly, I know I am in the van with Brothers Ribbon & his friends.

Are we dead? one of Brother's friends asks.

I don't think it happens that quick.

Yep, it does.

You took the curve too fast, Brothers.

Get up. See if we are dead.

I blow out the ancestors to hear what happened to us.

aaaahhhhhhhhh

eeeeeeeeeee

iiiiiiihhhhh

ooooooo

uuuuuuuuuuee

We are not dead.

There is a tail of light in our faces. The deputy laughs. You dumb asses got yourselves in a ditch again. I'll be back with the tow truck. Don't you Injuns worry.

We are giddy pretending to be dead. The opossum clan of our tribe.

Soon as the deputy is gone, Brothers starts his van. The men rock it back & forth. Their war cries scream. EEEEEEEEEEEEAUGH!

We fly down the road before the deputy & his men get back, the van dented like a face after smallpox. Brothers turns north on an old road, leaving heavy tracks, cuts into some tractor ruts through a field. He stops. One Indian gets out, stomp-dances on the road to cover our turn. They won't see it anyway, Brothers calls to him. Blind bats. Our heads hit the ceiling.

You got away! They shout.

How do you see in the dark? I ask, but Brothers is too busy driving. We turn back south on a county road. Once Brothers nearly turns over again. I scream & cannot help my screaming. Even I am not sure where we are.

Soon, I know the fork in the road & the next crossroads.
Soon we arrive at the old place. Brothers leaves his van
behind the house. There is one light at the back porch.
Someone throws a rock at it.

Turn out the light! I yell at them. Don't break it. Now I
have to buy a new light bulb. No wonder you Injuns are a
bunch of rucks.

The ride shook up the beer. I hear it fizz as they open the
keg.

Sister.

No, I say.

My brother tells me they are here to help me. As soon
as they know no cars are following me, he'll put in a new
light bulb.

You'll have to take one out of another socket, I tell
Brothers Ribbon. Besides, how could anyone find us? They're
probably still back at the bridge.

The men guffaw.

I know how unsteadily they laugh when confronted by
the deputy. How helpless they are before him. Their cackles
make no sense to me. I am disgusted with them.

They sit in the yard in the dark. A car comes down the
road, seems to slow, but passes. Their words speak with the
picket fence. What else could they say? Another car. They
talk again when it passes. The yard blooms moonflower &
nightshade in the dark the stars are clematis on the trellis
of the sky.

A car turns in the drive. Another. Lights come from
everywhere. Horns beat. We run crazy in the yard \ scream
\ SHOUT \ WAR WHOOP!

Attack!

I throw off boards in the junk pile. The ancestors moan. Their war cries fill the yard with the tremolo of their women.

Back to the cave where we were whittled off the Great Spirit. We call to Yehowah. Scrape off our silence & loss. We are brown sticks \ twisted limbs of pretzels. Give us your breath again.

ETOBAY.

The ancestors rampage from the corner of the yard where they stayed buried under the rubble. Sutata rises with his gun-stock war-club. Warriors & braves come up from the ground. The women ring-dance around the battle field.

The WARCRIES in the yard of the old house in the country. Abandoned. The place is mine if I can catch the universe running away as it does. Expanding into another sphere in which I do not yet fit, but for the ancestors SCREAMING in the yard to drive off the deputy & his men.

Eye bay cay tose hey ney.

EEEEEEEEEEEEOOOOOOOOOOHHHHHHHHHH!

They soon run.

Brothers! Brothers! I hear his moans. I sift through the men in the yard. I put my finger into their Indian parts. See, we are lovely, I tell them. Not the magnolia heavy with eyelids, but the frail, clinging clematis. We are a divided people, from under the rubble in the yard & from the sky.

Even far out in the heavens where the dead tribe migrated past stars. It is what great-grandfather tells his shriveled daughter on her deathbed laid out in the house where we visited her, drove miles with my brother & me impatient in the backseat sometimes fighting until my father stopped the car & knocked us in the head. Then we were quiet for a ways wiping our noses & sniveling.

The smell of his crotch reached our noses as we stood beside him at her bed. Hot & sweaty from the trip.

Pote Ey Yomo.

She is talking with her father, he told us. Our ancestors do not go away but keep coming on horseback & in rivulets of wagons from across the heavens & from under the rubble.

While she stayed in bed, her eyes migrated over the ceiling where she strung stars on the trellis, looking over the vast plains. Her stick trying to hurry us along like an old dog loaded with a small bundle. But we are awkward & stubborn & take our time.

Shittle. Grandmother's one word spoken for the year. No, I put my hand to her mouth & my mouth to her hollow cheek, try to send the word back into her ear so she can say it again before we leave.

I have no eyelids either, grandmother, see the stars cling like clematis on your trellis.

Hanka wa. HANKA WA.

The tribe follows the tracks of an elk herd nibbling the grass.

Walk one foot two foot walking.

Gentle hoof of the grazing herd.

Head up.

Eyes look.

Nothing sees.

Down grazes up looks.

Their pretzel horns shiny as varnish with salt crystals on the twisted curves.

Rum bah bah.

The ping of buckshot into roadsigns.

We can face destruction & be left standing, I tell the men as they crawl from the yard into the house. We can know we are here. We can come to the end & still go on in that black box of a kitchen where I wear a black dress with yellow buttons & search for a light bulb to quiet the squalling children of the slaughtered tribe. Old elk herd tramping through the walls. Yellow buttons on their eyes as I turn on a light.

We can be clobbered, fall to the ground. Rise. YOTE U EY, they say, RELEASE.

The Voluble Rap

THE PULL TOY SNAPPED UNDER HER FOOT. HER ANKLE TWISTED and she fell sideways, catching herself against the wall, enraged that she'd stepped on a toy left on the floor. The snares of children. The red devils. They could take you in. She picked it up and slammed it against the wall. Two more round yellow wooden wheels popped off and flew through the air. "Damn it," she screamed. "Damn!" Now the children would wake. She'd waited all day for them to be in bed. Now she probably had them up again—

Sure enough, they screamed. Two girls. A boy. "Shut up," she yelled at them. "All of you. It was your toy left on the floor that I tripped over. A damned yellow pig on wheels! Don't one of you come out of that room. This is my time. You had your day."

They whimpered for a while, the little one still screamed, but she knew the others would try to quiet her. How they had had their day. She paid the care center this morning, went to work, picked them up afterwards. Fixed their supper, which they picked at, walked them to the ice cream store. Brought them home with dripping cones, gave them a bath, got the dirt out of their hair, put their clothes in the washer, even read them part of a story. Then she covered them up and turned out the light.

Now IT WAS HER TIME.

Tomorrow would be the same, but she was without money but for a few dollars. She would have to charge gas and probably food before she got paid again. And they'd pass a toy store and tell her that's where they could buy some toy or bike they'd seen on television or somewhere in the neighborhood, though in the government housing she was in, there weren't too many new bicycles or toys to be seen. She didn't have the money. She'd told them a hundred times. The little suckers didn't understand. They kept gnawing on her like the dogs chewing on a bone. They also wanted a dog but she didn't have the money for that either. They begged constantly until they made her scream at them to shut up and she'd have another dream of them eating her—starting with her toes, up the calves of her legs, onto her thighs. That's usually the time she found she woke—about 3:00 and it was usually because she had to go to the bathroom. They hadn't eaten her after all, the little cannibals. They were sleeping in their beds unless they were sick or had a nightmare and she would have to rock them back to sleep or let them come in her bed.

Then she'd go to work groggy in the morning and would have to work all day and put up with their complaining and asking and fighting again that evening. Her boss consumed her just as her children did. In fact, sometimes she thought he was one of them, if she didn't look closely, he was there with the children eating her legs, sucking her substance—using her for his own profit and giving her little in return. Just enough to get barely across the bridge—but not quite, and each week before her paycheck, she'd fall into the river below.

The minute her check came it would be gone with rent and groceries and gas and utility bills and the child care center and usually a doctor bill because one of the children had been sick—or else she looked at the list of things they needed—shoes or underwear or overalls—it never stopped and she would NEVER have enough and she would have to decide which necessity to buy and which not to—and what about what she wanted—she ached at times for a new dress or a meal out. But there was not even money to keep up with the very basics they needed to survive and the greedy little cannibals consumed more of her each day.

"You fuckers stay in bed—" she could not control herself. Her anger spurted liked an overheated engine. Shit, she remembered. She owed for car repairs—only the necessary repairs—like brakes so the car would stop. Then shit! Their birthdays were coming—all in a row. In the meantime her old car would smoke and gurgle at stop lights and she would get nasty looks and sometimes even comments from someone because her car was polluting the atmosphere.

"If I hear one foot on the floor I'm going to cut it off. Then I'll beat you for getting the room bloody." She had hit them once before until she couldn't stop. The rage sometimes burned a hole in her. She was saddled with so much weight. She remembered slamming the door of the room the time she had been so harsh with them and crying in her own room for most of the night.

She was still in the hall. She would hold the door closed if necessary. She remembered her father's death for some reason. It was the same white hall she stood in—but these were not the nights she had stood in that hall nor stood at her father's bed as he grew weaker. Five weeks it took him to die and they all knew he was dying. And it was something he didn't want to do. And at the last she stood by his bed holding his hand that climbed and fell in air like a little car that would almost make it to the top of the hill and roll back down again.

Now these children she raged at would stand at her bed someday when she gasped for air the way he did and then take in less and less as though she were in an invisible airtight bag no one could see nor open and finally FINALLY the rasping breath would stop. Only they would look down and say, "good riddance!" to her. "That is the woman who used to scream at us and drive her fingernails into our arms while we screamed for mercy. That's the hateful mother who never did anything for us but screw up our lives. Let's divide her bones."

Maybe she had not loved them properly, disciplined them properly. She let them get away with what they wanted until her anger flared and then it was too late to discipline with firmness. It was rage by then. They made her life miserable. They were a hole in the ground she could never fill. That must have been the way her husband felt, and finally left because he knew whatever he did, it would never be enough.

She felt her ankle throb and held her hand around it a

moment. It would hurt at work tomorrow. Then with the foot that didn't hurt she kicked at the roll-pig now without its wheels.

She remembered the mother she'd seen with four children in the restaurant where she worked. They sat politely at the table and ate their meal. Her kids would have been all over the place. It would have been a little bit of hell to sit with them in a restaurant. Even the one she worked at. Why was the unrest and turbulence always in her house? How could she get out of it? Was there was no way?

She was wrapped up tightly in the housing development where she lived. The air being used up each day until finally she would suffocate the way her father did. Though he didn't really suffocate, the air hunger he had at the end was as if he did. He had looked so much like his mother when he died—as though he entered her again as he had once departed from her into this life—would she look like him when she left?

"Daddy," she wanted him back. He had been a good parent. But her children would not say that of her when they saw her dead—no, they wouldn't. They would say, this is our mother who laid down on the road and let the world run over her and we had a childhood of hardship. Fuck them.

Still the undercurrents of the house ravaged her. Her husband an ostrich with his head in the sand. She didn't know where he was most of the time though he tried to send child support. He was her former husband. She had to start thinking of him in those terms. He would never be her husband again. He would never know what the responsibility of children was. He'd hit out since the first—drunk of weekends—then absent for longer periods. He was probably drunk somewhere this minute in some woman's arms while she had the burden of the family on her shoulders.

She pressed her head against the battered wall so hard her forehead burned. She was nothing in this world. A minus number in the algebra book she'd had in school and could never understand, but that's what she was. She couldn't do anything. Her shyness kept her from seeking work of any importance. She was even afraid of waitressing and always lacked assurance. She had no skills like the pretty women who moved about the city in their sports cars, dropping off their children at the care center in such a hurry, running off to this meeting or that luncheon or important appointment, while she hobbled in to the care center, the stink of her car going in the door with the children. The looks of people at her—and she knew already what each moment of her day at the restaurant would be— she would be on her feet hustling with people's orders for eight hours. No one important wanted to see her.

She had nothing—not even money to get to another place to look for a better job. Her children oppressed her. Her dead father, her sick mother. Her former husband in the arms and between the legs of another woman. Probably starting another family with someone else while she was left holding the bag. Maybe he would finally be strapped with children the way she was. She hoped so.

But where was the fault? The children, herself, her former husband, parents, civilization itself, or the rolling pig that had been underfoot? None alone seemed to bear the blame. Maybe it was a little of them all. She shuddered.

It was in this very hall that her husband had raged sometimes when he was drunk or drying out from a drunk. He had pounded holes in the wall in his rage while she hovered in the children's room with them hoping they wouldn't be next. She could see the irregular bulges in the plaster where he'd fixed the holes he made. Right next to them was the nick she'd made with the pull toy. The scars showed up more under the ceiling light than in daylight. The hall was always dim in the day anyway. He had felt oppressed by his job in which there was nothing but degradation and routine, and he felt oppressed by his family—his wife ALWAYS asking for something he couldn't provide and three screaming banshees NEVER satisfied either—Oh god, maybe they'd died and were in hell because of their sins—oh god, where was the Great Spirit of the fathers, who, when they roamed the plains, endured and grew large within themselves in the act of migration— until they were wiped out with this ridiculous civilization.

And no matter how hard she prayed nothing ever changed. "DEAF GOD!" she screamed in the hall. "DEAF AND DUMB GOD!!"

"If you bastards don't leave me alone I'm going to walk out of this house and go to Albuquerque and NEVER come back and leave you to starve." She heard the children still whimpering. "I'm tired of you sucking me dry." She was screaming again now. "I hate working! I hate cleaning house and doing laundry at night. I hate cooking for you bastards."

Maybe soon she would be like her father pulling the curtain down on the pullman he rode out of Oklahoma when he died. Maybe if you struggled long enough—you could finally pull the curtain down. Maybe that's what he was doing with his hand when he was in the coma just before his death. Though he never screamed at her the way she did at her children.

"I don't CARE, god, if you IGNORE me ALL my life," she cried with her forehead still pressed to the wall and her whole foot throbbing. "I don't care if you leave me to lick crumbs off the floor forever, I believe in GOODNESS though I've never seen it. I'm going to believe in GOD!"

Holation

"THE FULL SKIRT OVER HER ROUND HIPS—LIKE CURB-FEELERS ON my '56 Ford—I remember those things about her," Joseph Stink, the Indian hermit, said. "But when I found she'd been moving on sometimes without me—and civilization with her—I came to this cabin. There wasn't any way I could go on like I wanted to."

"A lot of us feel that way," I told him.

"I study words, try to learn a new word each day," Stink confided. "Whee beaken who choo. Now that one I heard in my sleep. It's a train from its separate cars, or a runaway horse from its herd. Sometimes I even spell them backwards—"

I looked at my toenails.

"Cull—something selected to be removed. That's my word for today," he told me.

I thought for a minute. "You mean like 'lluc?' Or you mean you've got to cull your words when you hear a lot of

them—" I hoped he would get my message so I wouldn't
have to make it any clearer that I thought his canoe was
sideways in the current.

I didn't want to come here, but Stink had written for the
paper once, and I had to talk to him.

"Hoyden is a rude girl. But that wasn't Hannah. No, she
had grace." He paused. "Pedate means feet. That was one
of my old words. One I have ready to use whenever I need
it." He paused. "Others are still in the book just
waiting—"

Should I be taking this down?

"Holus bolus," he went on. "All at once all together." He
looked at me and lit a huge cigar. "Holophotal—an apara-
tus used in a lighthouse—" he read, "by means of which
light is collected and thrown in certain directions."

I saw his other dictionaries on the desk, his notebooks
and journals, scraps of paper, pencils, the whole cache of his
sacred writings.

"Hymen," he said. "Humpback. Hunger. I like the h's."
I got the new drift of his thought.

"I tired of travel after a while though," he said. "Bugs
and road tar was all I ever got in the grill of my Ford. I
bought it new in Okemah. Loaded with mudflaps. Front
aerials. Back antennas. Wire hubs. Hannah used to clean
the car for me after our trips. That's all I asked her to do.
But after a while we had fewer dollars to count out at all-
night filling stations and hash houses and we wondered
what it was all about." He paused. "The white man even
took migration away from us."

I scratched my neck.

"Hannah loved to travel—we could start out in the morning not knowing where we were going and by 11 or 12 o'clock at night we felt like we'd gotten there. Sometimes we'd camp out along the road. There's a place in travel—a sedentary sense of being in a real place. If I can make myself clear—travel in itself is a place."

The cigar in his mouth looked like a horse penis.

I wrote stories, biographies, essays and fragments for the newspaper. The column had lost its jazz, the editor said. I had to find Joseph Stink, who wrote back in the forties when he and Hannah were hotfooting it around the country—though the editor didn't mention Hannah. It was back to the roots for the column. I was supposed to learn something—if I wanted to keep my job.

This guy was a character and his writing had been outrageous. Maybe that's what drew readers to him. "Are you sure you're not here in this isolated cabin writing a novel—fiction seems to fit you—"

"Whay doo," He said, or something like that. "Naw—I only wrote articles for the Tulsa journal. Only the real stuff. Drawings on the cave wall, etc."

"That's what fiction is—the real stuff made to sound as if it wasn't."

"I think you got it the other way around, son," Joseph Stink said. "Something not real made to sound like it were."

"Son?" I asked. "I'm a woman."

"Oh, that's right. So you are. I guess I don't have my glasses on. Your hair is whacked off so short and you're wearing trousers—you got to be understanding about mistakes like that."

"Sure," I said.

Personable, I guess. If you liked skunks. I looked at his one-room cabin, with a table he must have made from a shed door. He had two chairs, an unmade bed, a lantern, jars of fruit on the table, an Indian calendar on the wrong month where Chief Standing Bull or someone stared from the wall as though he were in a dentist's chair.

"Good buddy," I said. Horse teeth and all. Corn kernels of his eyes—yellowish. Stink himself was rustic as his place. "I've got to hear more about what it was you put into your articles which the editor is hankering for me to get a handle on."

"Those long nights under the stars stretched out with Hannah made the trips. The others I traveled with—not so. Yeah, she was worth her oats. Nothing like her when she wore her flea-market fur, a green velvet dress she had and a veiled hat. She had this beaded bag she carried—" He thought about it a moment and slapped his knee. "What a little heifer. You know what she wanted to do? She wanted to travel to pow wows and festivals. She wanted to make hanger art! She'd seen crumpled hangers in a flea mar-ket—said they were better than any sculpture she'd seen. What a hammerjack! That's what she always used to talk about—hanger art. Yep. She did."

It must have been a blast.

"Gee-unny! How that woman thought. Some of that stuff I wrote was from what she said. She kept talking how we could travel to street markets—even Sante Fe—and sit on our blankets and sell the hangers she twisted to look like silos a plane sat on, or haystacks struck by lightning. She would use the old hangers that had rusted—almost like barbed wire and the little hook at the top would hang them any place you wanted— Ognib! How her eyes were afire when she talked. Buy up all the old hangers and start twisting. I come close to marrying that woman. A strong-willed—if it hadn't been for her talk about all them hangers."

"Well, what happened to her if you were so fond of her?" I asked.

"Holus bolus. She left. Someone else picked her up—another traveling man—rodeo or horse-roper," he paused. "A bull-rider probably. I couldn't compete with that. She got expensive too and talked all the time about hangers. So I trudged on with my language— Finding a new word to use each day. It keeps a man busy."

"I suppose," I said. "But I have to find more than one word a day. The editor remembers you with fondness," I told Stink.

"Sometimes I use them on the women who come to cook for me. Don't keep them too long either." He puffed on his long cigar. "Can't tell it from the way I talk, but those words are in my head—"

I knew that Joseph Stink was an authority on the commonplace—the migration of geese and deer herds. What the universe in general was doing at any given moment—

"I'm plowing now—" he said, "so these widows can get in their vegetable gardens. But civilization hightails it away from me. It crosses the road when it sees me coming."

I made a few more notes.

"I been a guide for the white fishermen and hunters, helping the animals get away from them mostly—telling the fish when to stay under the logs near the creek-bank."

There was a "No Trespassing" sign nailed on his house. Also "Beware of Dog." His old mutt half-dead—he hadn't even barked at me. The sign should say, "Beware of Joseph Stink."

"Well, I used to wait for a letter from Hannah every day. But she was slow with her writing and eeooo—she couldn't spell. She almost wrote backwards. She probably had no stationery nor pen and was too busy trying to catch her rodeo man. Once she wrote on a piece of grocery sack. I don't blame her. But she was one of the sweetest pastures you'd find."

Was he telling me anything I needed to know?

"Yeah, I woke up one time when I was a boy—the room was full of mottled light like the moon had just squeezed through the window. This light was whitish as an eyeball that couldn't see. No, I think it was more of a balloon or a tooth from—"

At that, a small piece of laughter burst from my mouth. I didn't know what to make of this guy.

"Gee oo," he said. "You don't laugh at giant teeth when you wake up and find them in your room."

"I guess not."

"But it was them sorts of things from the beginning when I was a boy, I knew I saw things different than others. I only told my mother once what I'd see, and Hannah not hardly more than once either—"

He scratched his head and I rubbed the eraser into my note pad.

"It was actually my python that brought the teeth to my room— Later—not when I was a boy. Toby my python. He's gone now. I used to keep him in those bottles on that shelf up there on the wall. I got to drinking whiskey regular and soon Toby moved in and we were friends for a long time. Now Hannah never cared for him. Her father had been a drinker too and she wouldn't have anything to do with the stuff." He took the cigar between his fingers and wiped his mouth. "She wouldn't have anything to do with me either when I got to yelling at Toby."

I must have showed my shock because he went on about something else.

"I used to live around Wildhorse, Oklahoma, which isn't there anymore. There's just a boarded up filling station like a turtle on the side of the road."

Toby the python. I turned it over in my head.

"I think it was his teeth I used to see. When I was seeing teeth. But an empty bottle will not hold him. You got to keep drinking."

"I suppose," I said.

"I used to clean up barns—nothing like shoveling manure. I think that's why I liked my column. Actually, it was gas for the Ford. Otherwise, Hannah and I would be stuck at home and that's one place Hannah didn't like to be." He smiled to himself a moment— probably remembering the full skirt around her round hips and all. "I used to polish the hames and traces and horse-collars and bits." He puffed again on his horse-penis. "Hannah was like waiting for a catalogue order which never arrived."

There were some awkward spaces of silence between us.

"Now one of my stories was about an embalmed body left in a funeral parlor for several years." Joseph started on another tale. "There was a picture of him in the museum in

Pawhuska and I did a story—Hannah sitting there with some little girl—cutting out paper dolls with blunt scissors—in a plaid flannel shirt and white blouse. I could hardly keep my eyes off her."

I was thinking it was nearly time to go.

"I wrote about a tornado too—the brown cloud across the sky like a buffalo head with lightning-arrows shooting from his eyes. I took a giant step after him when the earth turned hollow like it does—a real roller-coaster in the twisted sky—" He leaned forward in his chair with exaggerated movements of his arms. "I'm surprised it didn't start Hannah on the hanger art again. Maybe she said something about twisters and how it would fit—if I would make a small investment in her business."

I remembered his tornado story. He'd nearly been killed. Someone remarked that he must be a genius, but I thought he was a helter-skelter old man.

"Somewhere once we were in an abandoned adobe." He started talking again. "Hannah and I made love while the room sucked evening light through the windows like they were nipples—"

"Damn that man," I said under my breath, "and his blasted talk about Hannah." Why did he think I'd care about them making love?

"The editor wouldn't print that story." He said. "It was one of my best—Hannah beside me with a red scarf around her waist like a chili, billets of old rodeos and pow wows on the wall, the small flame of the Coleman flickering like it was burning a doorway between her bones."

"Ahhhhmm," I cleared my throat and thought he still had to be writing. This guy was a poet! A little seedy—but he sure could set a scene.

"Mr. Stink, I don't see how the juicy details of your affair with Hannah could possibly mean anything to me. Would you get on with it?" I asked.

What was he saying? Should I go on the road irresponsibly, sleeping about the country, taking up with Toby the python?

He looked at me a moment. "I had the feeling you were here to talk man to man—"

"Not exactly." I had noticed Stink's car in the yard—mudflaps, aerials, curb-feelers and all—weighted down like a thousand-pound grasshopper ready to pounce—I asked him about the car to have something to alter the course of our conversation.

He didn't say much.

"What's in the trunk?" I asked.

"The field rocks are still there, I suppose." He said, "I'm going to build a path to the outhouse and woods. I've tripped there several times at night. There's a spring where I cool watermelons. The last several times I fell I dropped the melon. There's nothing I like better than to plop a watermelon into the spring. It sinks and bobs and finally gets cold enough for the ladies and me to eat—the ones who come to do some cooking for me. Sometimes of an evening we have watermelon and talk. It's nothing like it was with Hannah—when she left there was no one to fill her place. But the others will do to talk to— The watermelon in the spring makes me think maybe we got to do the same thing—sink and bob in this life til we get cool enough to appeal to someone—"

If I got his drift—he might be telling me something.

"I ought to be more pedate?" I said.

"At least on your toes."

"Ognib." I thought. "How long the rocks been in your car?" I asked.

"Several months. I was going to get to them once but it seemed Hannah came back. I could feel her in that green velvet dress here in the room with me. I think she needed something and I tried to go to her—well, I woke up and it was morning and I didn't get it done. Then one thing came up and another and them rocks are still in the back of my car." Stink walked to the window and stood there for a while, growing more silent the longer he stood.

"Give me another word for the day—" I tried to revive him.

"Holation," he answered soon. "Spreading of a light beyond its boundaries."

I looked at him.

"It's like the light coming in a window can seem bigger than it actually is."

"Are you talking about Hannah? Or is this another 'wild tooth in your room at night' story?"

"It's up you to, young woman, make of it what you want."

I watched the horny man as he stood at the window.

"Do we cull this conversation?" I asked.

"A tu ne pah," he answered.

"What are those words you always say?" I asked.

"Those are my vocables. They don't have to mean anything."

"All right," I said. "I understand."

I was getting ready to leave when he started talking again—

"There she is again—Hannah. The thought of her comes through my head. I hardly know. Those constellations starting to come out now are sometimes the wire hangers she puts up there."

I looked at the sky.

"It's as though she has her booth up there and she finally got her way. And you and I are down here looking up at the work she sets out. Yes ma'am, I know that's where she'd be if she had a choice."

I stepped back from Stink a moment and looked at him while I still had the chance. I think I learned about watermelons in the spring from him; if he had his way, we'd step in—get our feet wet, sink, rise, and bob sometimes not knowing which way we were going— Had I been as stuffy and pedantic as he seemed to think?

And was he as lonely at the window as he looked?

No, I thought—it's just the way things were—he had found something he wanted to hold on to, and he held on as long as he could. Now he was telling me to capture the same sense of migration to a real place—taking I-19—B-2—the road growing larger all the time.

Regretfully

THE CAT SITS WITH ME THIS MORNING WHEN SLEEP LEAVES LIKE love for the man I married & lived with 19 years until love puckered, shriveled to pit & seeds of grapes & melon. This morning sleep steps away too early like a person from the room or the company of one I once wanted to stay. Now I am awake in darkness. The clunk of paper on the porch. The alimony check left under the door. The cat's legs tucked under, her head bowed as one of the manger animals.

What is it she thinks when she stares at the wall \ bookcase \ coffee mill \ water color of the Black Mesa \ gouache of an Indian blanket?

Out of the silence \ the airplane & city noise \ the bluejay's shrill bark.

The ragged edge of fire was a sawblade in our last winter together when bones crushed into fertilizer for the zinnias & marigolds. Only the hardy flowers for this climate.

You lost wife & job \ married again \ look for another job. I will stay with the child who stayed in the house with you so she could remain in the same school. Now she does not want to go with you as I did not want to go. When you leave I will move back into our territory. Pay too much rent. What choice is there?

You say, what the shit. Child support, lawyer's fees. We are whipped before we start. I left your drunken romp in the rude leaves. I could not stay.

You are someone to whom commitment was made, in whose bed \ I slept 20 years. What do you want?

You kept the house, the furniture, savings, now they belong to you & the new wife & I am left chewing the jerky of this trail. I hear men say how they lost all they had. I am the same after divorce. My property settlement in monthly payments \ you are tired of not two years later. We jab, pinch, poke one another.

The cat sits by me this morning I cannot sleep. You are the locust she carried yesterday in her mouth, laid on the floor for me to see. It squeaked like a proud man without a job & a young wife you must satisfy or lose again.

This beast in me wants to pull off your wings, bite into your ass, butt you with my paw until you walk sideways in helpless hysteria.

You say I cause a heart attack but you bring it on yourself. The cat stares at the bookcase. Wooden spools from grandmother's sewing basket \ thread gone \ these artifacts she left \ the dark wicker \ the bright beads on the frayed lid.

& yet there are enough predators in this life. I want to live with dignity. I want a strange reverence for this failed life I feel.

Church bells in the early morning dark. The cat beside me desires nothing for the moment. Later she will prowl, bring in the tail & back legs of a small mouse \ the headless baby bird \ the cruelty with which each animal day goes by.

In the stillness I peel away the layer of years like the tight skin of grapes. Uncovering the seeds of the first years we lived together. Somehow not together the way we should be. You with your job, the children were mine. Once we went to the zoo & your anger there over nothing angered me. The memory stalks my head like corridors in the monkey house.

The books from my years in school, pictures from trips, portraits of family above the bookcase. A cow's skull I found in the grasslands of western Oklahoma, prairie weeds standing in a jar. Rocks. Some of them my father gave me before he died. We had the same habit of picking them up. A worn brick from an old street in a small Kansas town. Birds' nests. A flowered couch upon which I sit with my cat. The semé chairs.

In the trunk, where I rest my feet, a brown bear, drawings by the children, the collection of the second 20 years of my life, vacant as two cat eyes. Pointed ears \ the long tail of counsel I have given myself \ a pewter bowl from our marriage on an early May evening when we were young & awkward & not prepared for a single-bottom plow on a field cankered by weeds & red clay.

I hissed & growled at you \ tore the wall between us \ left \ & know we are still bound.

It is as though I live near the dark morning you inhabit but could never enter. & I screamed at you that I have the responsibility but not the fun of marriage \ throwing off my imprisonment \ my own capture \ I stayed with you years longer than I wanted to & your sad eyes looked at me regretfully when I said I was no longer your wife.

It was too hard for me \ my father's death, your rantings, our son's surgeries, then my mother's. I couldn't always swallow my anger like the bowl of melons on the table. This vacancy you left me. I regret your neglect of me. Your early lessons of expedience & compromise. I would have learned them anyway.

The cat sighs \ her little sides heave \ she stretches when I rub her back. She curls up like a withered petunia beside my newspaper & coffee. Her counsel is to stare at the bookcase & wall, the trunk of children's drawings, the basket of empty spools, the thread somewhere in old clothes hanging in secondhand stores. She pulls at the button on my robe, curls up again.

Fussing like clucking squirrels I hear in the tree, I cannot change my feelings. A distant siren. A neighbor starting his car. The squeak of the roll-away in the other room. Strata of rock on the Black Mesa slant like early rain falling on the prairie.

I watch the chimney broom \ the grapevine wreath & read the paper.

Soon the sun rises moist as the melon in my hands. The slick wet seeds spill through my fingers. I hold the soft bear in the trunk \ the baby I once rocked \ the young husband I once had.

The Orchard

BILL NAVAT WOKE THAT SATURDAY WITH THE DREAM OF APPLES.
Through the trees, the morning sun speckled the wall.
He turned a moment and looked at his wife. She was still
asleep; probably dreaming also before she woke.

A thin image of his dream spread itself inside his
forehead again, feeling moist as the white inside of apples.
He dozed momentarily. It was an orchard, probably one
he'd seen long ago. Small patches of sunlight flickered from
the window.

He came to consciousness again, firmly now, and got up.
Maybe it was the cold autumn. He shut the window, quietly
not to disturb her, and went downstairs.

Apples, he thought. Had he once eaten too many? Had
he dreamed he was a boy climbing an apple tree in his
backyard at the farm? Had he been in an orchard somewhere recently? Something must have reminded him of
apples. There was a hard, round image pushing into his

head again, a definite surge of his will. His mouth watered
with the thought of tartness. Maybe he was only hungry.
Small brown holes in the apples, freckles. A dried leaf on
the stem.

He ran water into the coffeepot, thought he would like
an apple fritter, one he remembered from childhood, but his
wife didn't bake. She worked and was busy with the
children—their music lessons and art lessons. He let her
sleep on Saturday. She might rather stay in the kitchen and
cook fritters, but she had to work. His salary as director of
Indian exhibits at a museum didn't stretch far enough, and
he remembered the fritters. A cold blue wedge of morning
sliced the corner of the table. Shiny apples, red as sumac.
He walked the edge of consciousness where images dance.

A man's hard voice called from the barn. He heard it in
his head. The memory of it embedded his daydreaming.
The harsh cold mornings he tried to shrink back into sleep
startled him. Close the large and creaking door. Some
neighboring farmer always disgruntled. Bill vowed then he
would not let his life close in on him so that he felt cornered,
and could only lash out with an ugly voice at his wife and
children.

He remembered the chickens in a tree on the shed roof.
The one time the creek flooded and his father sold the farm
in eastern Oklahoma and they moved to Carthage, Mis-
souri. Bill's father didn't let things close in on him. He got
out in the yard and danced in a circle. He acted out what he
had to do in the ceremonies passed down from the ancestors. Bill could follow them too. Yes. That's the way life was.

Bill wondered what had happened to the disgruntled
farmer. He probably still yelled from the barn.

In Carthage, there was an orchard down one street and up another. One of those old houses with some land between new tracts of houses in the surburbs. An owner who wouldn't sell to developers, but stayed until new houses surrounded him, retreating behind overgrown firs and bushes.

The morning light streaked the wall of the kitchen. Neighboring children would soon appear at the door to ask if his children could play. He thought of the path into the old orchard, already his sides ached. He poured a cup of coffee and made toast. He sat at the table and thought about the job he had been offered at a museum in New Mexico and he wanted to bolt. But he was settled where he was, though the walls of the small, private gallery closed in about him and his hands were tied by curators who wanted to keep it as it was and had always been.

His wife liked her job. His children were satisfied in school. He was a holy man in the Indian Church, a leader in the sweat lodge ceremony. His job at the museum was secure. He liked to walk along the display cases and show the feathered coup sticks, the baskets and blankets and spears he had arranged—the buffalo hunting-mask he had purchased for the museum—the tortoise-shell leg rattles and ceremonial gourds. Yes, he had done well. Why should he want to leave familiar surroundings for some distant museum in the desert?

He made a circle dance on the table with his fingers, walking them around and around. He would stay in one place. The migrations had ceased. He remembered the times he had gotten on a bus and ended up someplace far away. Calling back home for money to return. Where had it gotten him? He had to part with those ways.

He was from a small woodland tribe. His father had been able to farm. What would he gain by leaving? What did he know about southwestern Indians? The tribes were so different. He poured another cup of coffee and returned to the table. He read a letter left open from a relative— Uncle Redwing, one his wife intended to answer. His seeds in the core of her, their children asleep, or maybe awake, watching cartoons in their room. They had watched television late last night and had gone to sleep. He had wakened in the night, he remembered, and gone in to find them sleeping; the programs off for a while, the static filling the room, the milky face of the television like a sore moon through the dark.

The apple pushed itself into his consciousness again as an unwelcome guest, a reminder of what he didn't want to be reminded of: he had a will to run, to disobey, that whacked at him sometimes with an ax. How many workers had been fired at the museum? They showed up for a while, then wouldn't come on time. He had to get over that urge to drift. He would stay in one place! Unless there was reason to leave. That's what the world required. He had invested too much of his life where he was.

He heard other children playing outside though it was still early. He didn't want his children to come downstairs yet. He wanted to sit at the table by himself and think. He wanted to walk his fingers around the table in one place again. He was restless at the museum, but a man didn't leave his job. The curators praised him; he ran the museum with precision.

The moon was an apple without a core. Where was his core? Directing Indian exhibits in a museum? Discussing the collection at ladies' luncheons? Why wasn't he satisfied? Sometimes the world closed in on a man. But he would stay. He would pull himself away from that urge to bolt. He made his fingers circle in one place.

Besides, wouldn't he find the same old discontent in a new place?

He heard his children upstairs, their brown eyes flecked with seeds. What if his wife knew he kept the company of apples? he thought as he took one from the bowl. He turned the apple in his hand. It had the roundness of the earth. The core made a star when cut crosswise through its girth. He remembered the red coil of peel when his mother pared apples like the vision of a spirit horse with braided mane. He used his fingers as though they were legs. He got on the horse. Let's go, he said. He'd ride in place. Yes. That's the journey he'd make.

In This Mission School

1.

I HEAR THE VOICE OF MY MOTHER WHO LEFT ME: DUBBUE, SHE cries, daughter of Willing Horse who went somewhere with an ache in his side.

The wood floors scraped with our feet, a blade of someone we see in a book who walks on ice. SKATE that word called by those who have-the-house.

You can understand hard water, I say. It is the yolk when it has its claws & beak.

We listen to Miss Nolly Terrick in the morning mission school where the earth is yellow as the yolk I beat into the bowl. She talks of math & geography. The beak & claw not yet formed. The hard kernel somewhere in the stalk.

She is never quiet, never still. In the afternoon, she moves our laziness from one corner of the mission school to the other. We dust, wash our clothes, sweep, sit dumbly in

the school row. She has to be over someone & chooses us.
She kicks our legs so she can heal our shin bones. One
cough & she shovels the burning coal of medicine into our
throats. The fire-barrel by the ice-hard water. A handkerchief if we choke. At night, she has the punkah, a canvas
frame suspended from the ceiling to fan her room.

She cannot stand our quiet. Yet she must have us as the
brood for her empty corner of the field. Where is our house
in this not-house-having? Our claw in the yolk?

Dubbue. I hear my mother's voice in the night. Tonka
wah. Where are you?

Straws in a box in the corner of the kitchen where the
woman moves, a sow with piggies clamped on her teats.

Oh, yes, Miss Terrick knows the sun pops up like toast
to warm her hands. She snuffs the crumbs, touches with
delight the sow-veins on her legs. She wallows in the sty of
the kitchen, smiling in the one warm corner she finds in the
whites of her little piggies' eyes.

Miss Nolly Terrick in her Betha-collared dress talks to
us in the early morning dark. She shakes the rudeness in
our heads where buffalo graze & moving tribes stalk.

Where is the grace of your mother, Dubbue? Sit up
straight so that when she lets go of my head it jumps like
a rabbit from the brush in the dry creek-bed.

We will see what there is to find in this not-house-
having. What mothered us? Who fathered?

Him-who-left-with-an-ache-in-his-side. Willing Horse.
And the mother whose voice I heard calling me left.

Dubbue, she says at night.

Miss Terrick takes me to see my father when I stampede for him one night.

Then I see him in the ward-bed. He speaks to me once, his voice with strange hope. In this mission school, our lives pulled from us like tape from the wound in his side where they looked for his ache. The black road-bed of his scar. The red skin beneath.

Oh salve.

Jehovah HEALER. Jehovah ROPHE, she squeals at his bed. Jehovah makes the air hard. He is the ice we cross on the blades of our feet, the one who has claws & beak.

Willing Horse, I cry.

I know in the night my father crosses the prairie, a buffalo robe on his back, a war shield in his hand. I know now I will be in this mission school a while.

Tonka wah, daddy buffalo, on the plains he calls, eyoo eyoo.

Don't look.

The road from his grave curves like a pig's tail.

Under our punkah—the heavens.

Eyaw. We are loosed from this earth—

Our-house in this not-house-having.

2.

One-Who-Follows came from the covers of my body grabbing at air, his hands frantic for the dark he'd known. He was not willing to suck the milk at first—almost indifferent to it.

Now they say he has ruptured & we will stay at the clinic again. It is the place they took my father, Willing Horse, into a room & sewed his hernia. They gave him medicine that made him wild. He floated back from the ceiling where he told me there were holes. He was going to leave, he said, but I did not understand. He had not been with us for a long time anyway.

At night he prowled the clinic until they tied him in bed.

Then he said the crucifix came off the wall. The man stayed there, suspended as always— but his cross crawled to the tin bed, sniffed covers like a coyote & licked up my father's wounds. The man on the wall didn't seem to know. It was as though he toe-danced—sleeping or thinking about something with his eyes on the floor.

My father said he could get up from his bed then—he walked to the wall & touched the man, who flinched as though startled. My father said that is when he saw himself & the man dance with arms outstretched, their feet crossed \ hey yey \ in a rabbit-hop. He thought at first their feet were tied together but it was the way they had to prance as though digging post-holes—rising higher toward the ceiling until they could get through.

Now in the clinic at the mission school, I tell them it is true. One-Who-Follows watches the ceiling & squeals as if it were a vast prairie where they hopped upside-down \ heh heh \ he calls across the distance, holding up his little fists, waiting for them to reach back & pull him through.

Trigger Dance

ROAN'S EYES LOOKED AT THEM FROM 20 MILES AWAY. YONTER. The light looked all that way.

Some quilt his wife worked on like the galaxy afloat on pond scum. A witch in the black night, scarf tied on top of her head makin' little coyote ears sticken up. Turkey red, grays, brown, the witch's hands spread out, her feet spread also like shoes on stick legs pointing east & west.

Gruto. Roan was a man. Some little turquoise ghost jumping at his side. "When I build a fire for the sweat lodge," Roan says, "I hear their voices—those who are struggling & rising—even those lost in their own way. They all chant the night song. I say nua nuh to the spirits—not yet. Don't close. We just started to get straightened up in the shed. We do. Naw. Yeu can't take it back. But it's what they're goint ter do. It's too late for anything else. Just help make the ride out a'here a little less final. Like it's more a road to another end. That's what we're here for. We worked hard to name the animals & trees & seeds. We listened too long just to learn & now yeu're going to take it? Don't fairly fit the squared way I thinken. But we got the power now to kill the earth—"

Roan is probably the only Cheyenne that talks with a drawl. All the time his eyes burn like those rocks he chucks in the pit of the sweat lodge just after they come out of the fire.

"Hain't fair." He goes on talking. "I don't know the names of the stars yet how they twist & turn like swallows up there. Whee shomay. Yeu just can't."

Now this is the Great Spirit that Roan is talking to—& his tribe of spirits—like He was a father & they were brothers sitting in the yard chairs beside him picking straws out of the cuffs of their pants. No one else would talk to Him like that.

Roan & two of his boys, Jake & Kollar, watch his wife & the scraps of cloth she sews up—calico & prints & such— blood red & brown—as though she had 4 hands. They sit in Roan's backyard just south of Lawton, Oklahoma, under a few trees, one with a hole in its trunk. They are surrounded by Roan's house, a few scrubby sheds, a sweat lodge frame, & some brush. Farther away, another house where Roan's sister, Weazel, & their father live—Roan scratching his head now as he thinks of his father who was always feeling like he was dying. & in the distance, the Wichita Mountains across the flat land where a few cotton fields roam beyond a pond.

"We can't give up," Roan says. "Not now. I got another son getting married & she got to finish that quilt for them to ward off the night spirits & our old dreams of the trail so the sadness won't seep in— We got to be strong. We got to suffer & to help this world. Though they don't know it, we do. They don't knowd out there we was praying for them this very morning."

"Who's getting married?" Kollar asked.

"Well, yeu, son. I feel it in my bones."

Kollar was half-pleased, half-shaken.

"This hain't going to be an easy ride to the end. Stars will fall like quilt patches & the black night will fold a tarp over us & we will be burdened & bowed over & the black witch night will dance & laugh—& only by our prayercries & our hanging on to nothing will we make it through what's come—"

"Yes, we been hanging on to nothing for some time now," his wife says.

"Now I dunno its name but it's the last stop. Turable. Yes. Gives me shivers from my toenails to the ruckus in my ears."

"That's earwax, Roan," Kollar says.

"That's strife of the earth, son, & this 'ere a trigger dance we do & yeu go shucking it off as something I have but yeu dun't."

Roan's wife hung her quilts on the clothesline behind them. Autumn leaves all over the yard.

"Yeu say it weren't nothing to worry about, but dad, yeu do."

"Make up yeur thinking which way the buffalo herd is moving, pa. We shouldn't have to take the day conflabing about it."

"Purple leaves at that & the birds flying west as though the earth got jerked around & they don't know it yet," Roan har-harred at himself. "& I hain't one to tell those puckers with all them wings flappin."

Roan's wife looked one way so quick & then the other yeu thought she had two noses. & that turquoise fart jumping up then down. "Waul, yeu just want to snerp his head off with yeur fingernail like a tick," she said.

"The wallop yeu give with that truck, Jake, nearly took my head off in that black night we drove through," Kollar said, remembering something outside Roan's backyard.

"A woman knitting booties spooks me. I had to get away—"

"Leaves like raspberries on that 'ere red quilt. Jambers. It lights my eye." Roan spumed looking at his wife's quilts. & it was his eyes 40 miles away like 2 little planets burning in his head.

Stained apron hanging on her belly, her tongue snapping like quilt pieces in her lap—like rocks just out of the fire, angry & red with heat & dancing stiff as grandpa's socks.

"What little mulberries yeu eat today yeur sides ache yeur mouth's all purple?" one son asks another. "Yeu're alone all the day & night cause Stinky Henson shot 2 of yeur dogs. What'd yeu take all them mutts for inter town anywayd?" Kollar asked.

Jake shrugged.

"Causing trouble. His gift to the world. Drawing eyes til yeu got eyeballs stuck all over yeur shirt. No, fact. Yeu do," Kollar said. "Eyeball Jake. We ought to call him that."

"Turnip seed yeu do."

The boys fought with words between themselves until the mother glared at them, eyes up from her sewing back

down to her lap. They shut up when she looked at them.
One made a fuck sign at his brother when she looked away
but she knew it. "Jake!" she yimpered.

Roan was back to his far thinking.

The woman made a black eyeball for the witch she was
sewing on the quilt. "I'm ready to go to the yonter anytime,"
she said to Roan. "If the end comes, hain't so bad. There
isn't much but the spirit. Everything that matters here is
between us & Him. Why else stay? Seems troubles &
matters I don't want anything to do with. I'm aware of Him
all the time—seems like that's where we belong. Yep. It do."

Roan looked at her some.

"I hunger to go back to the Father, Roan. It's not that I
mind it here with yeu—but, Whay. Yeu're aware of him all
the time too. I can see it in what yeu do. I can see it in what
yeu left undone. It can wait cause something more important is happening to yeu."

"Yeah, pa. Thert the truth," Jake mustered.

"Yep. We got to get sanding the chest, putting in the
drawers. We got to have somewhere to put our things. Not
in boxes under the bed the way Jake does. No. We goint t'
have a house to live in—with chairs & a table & drawers for
our socks. Yeu see. We do."

"All the eticut he's come into. What hintered him so
long?" Jake sputtered.

"Not having a woman," his ma said.

"That's what does it?" Jake asked.

"Surpost teh."

"Now if ma were sewing up the universe there doing it
her own way," Kollar went on, "a turquoise tree or a blue
one instead of the green or say, brown at the end of the dry

spell can yeu just imagine what the earth would look like, nothing the spirit would want to come home to."

"Nawp," Roan said.

"Well, Jake & pa," Kollar said. "There's got to be ordonnace. There's got to be a hand saying do it this way & not that. & all of yeu mind cause this one is the one keeping the whole in mind & not just the part yeu're working on at the moment. Otherwise we'd have kay-OS. Yerp. We would. & we don't want that."

"Wy nert?"

"I dern't know. It's just better to be setting here with order & dignity around us having things done right. & we's not to question just to obey & sand our drawers & plant our garden & heat up the rocks for the sweat lodge. Then it be over."

"Now yeu dern't gone & told me my whole life that was ahead of me & I wanted it to be a surprise." Jake hit his shoe & jammered to himself. "Daurs!" His dogs licked themselves in the yard.

Roan's wife looked at her son like he wasn't there at all but some horsefly bothering her nose. Then she sewed on another patch on her quilt that already looked at misery itself.

The sky rattled in a corner of it—

Its square clouds falling in. Clumps of sky bound up like newspapers to be thrown at the farmhouse or stuffed in the little tubes by the road.

"So we got to know someone's holding onto us as we fall like a black leaf to the night—" Roan stroked his eye—

"Gars." Jake remarked.

**

One black mother cloud came up in the west, but passed. A python neck all puffed out. Glaring tongue darted like lightning. "Something's got ahold of us but beyond that is the light. We're in the jaws of it." Roan talked to Gerp, his married son, who came with his small children to see how grandpa was feeling.

"So tell what you think is coming. I think the white man has a buffalo & it's being shot off. Just like the buffalo our tribes followed. Now. I can't say what this buffalo is, because I don't know. I don't live with them, but I feel there's a slaughter going on of something that's eroding the foundations where they stand." Roan stopped work on a rabbit cage for Gerp's children, who chased around the backyard.

"What can we do?"

"Nothing, I suppose. It's too late. The sky will fold up like a quilt & fall. The thread's unraveling even now & the land will turn over & the plague of locusts, like helicopters or bombers or missiles or whatever, will swarm the skies. We will have the spitting out of mountains & rivers & it will all rise up & walk off without us on it anymore. Heaven & earth will pass away. It's been passing away for some time now but no one noticed or if they did & spoke about it, no one listened. Well, it's that way, seems to me."

"Where will we go?" Gerp asked.

"We'll perish or go to the Great Spirit's heaven we believe in," Roan answered.

"Is that the way it is?"

"Haven't yeu been preached that to before?" Roan's wife interjected.

"Yes. I have but I can't say that I ever understood," Gerp answered his mother.

"Just give him 100 years or so," Roan said.

**

Jake trimmed his toenails with a hunting knife amid his dogs. His brother Kollar looked at him in his own thoughts.

Then Roan came to the backyard suddenly & started talking & then was silent again. His wife beside him not sewing this one time but looking off into the universe at the planets in their paths around the sun. Sometimes she says something like "Wa ah" to one of the angels flying there, maybe taking souls up or down.

"Jake, yeu're going to remove a toe if yeu aren't careful." Roan interrupted his thinking. "I'm getting squeamish just watching yeu jab at yeurself with the blade."

"I was jus thinkin' that" Kollar said.

"Yeu aren't supposed to whittle on yeurself like that—" & knowing Jake, his blood would shoot like a ballistic missile.

"Ain't t'nurther way to get this nail off. Id like a tin roof on a shed to curt into. Ain't coming off no way."

"Well, don't take the whole toe off just to get to the nail. I would say the Indian's close to God—" Roan went on talking in the same breath.

"Possibly," his wife said with a flyswatter in her hand.

"Saw himself trampled under the white foot of civilization, had it stuffed up his nose & his way of life shredded & he has nothing to go on & he can't say what it is he can't reckon."

"Maybe whom the Great Spirit loves he allows to wallow—was not his son ravaged on the cross that he would be a new man?" Roan's wife shifted in the yard chair—"& us wid him." She scratched her arm with the end of the swatter.

"Shutt." Jake said but there wasn't any blood. Just a crease in the hard yellow nail like petrified snot.

"It's more than we understand why we were overrun." Roan approached his thought again.

"Not so, really. The land is more than we could ever understand." His wife added light with a swat of her hand. "Oil & minerals & land cultivation. They'd still be there if it was up to us. & overrun with buffalo. Only killing what we need. We'd have been up to our ears in buffalo. Just think of the catastrophe they spared us."

"We wouldn't even had the horse nor gun without the white man," Kollar said.

"Ner whiskey, ner smallpox," she added.

"Ner salvation in Christ," Roan said.

"Maybe we'd be ruled by buffalo then, ma? Har. Nurver thoud of thad one. So many of them we'd just be trampled under foot. Ma, yeu always saw things yeur own way." Jake chummed.

"Naw—the son of the Great Spirit dying for us on a cross—we couldn't think that one up ourselves."

"Jake, if yeu don't take that knife away from yeur toe I'm going to take yeur tonsils out with it instead."

"Roan," he asked his pa, then tossed the blade down into the ground. Clicked his fingers as though he'd split a blade of grass. "Shupos—"

"We're talking too often," Kollar interrupted. "Maybe we been put here to know misery. Maybe someone just got to know it to complete the knowledge of humanity on earth & we're the ones chosen to know that."

Jake scratched his crotch.

"To live without our spirit," Roan said.

"Yerp," Jake answered.

"But why were we left when he came & took our land & squeezed us into a ground hog's burrow to live in all our lives & remember what it was when we had the sun creeping over our head & the spirit walking beside us clipping his toenails & talking to us right here among us."

"They didn't kill us all. Even a few buffalo are up the highway on the buffalo farm," Roan surmounted.

"Yeah, & aren't they kicking up their heels each day for being taken care of & gawked at by tourists who come to see just what kind of beast their ancestors killed off like they were flies or termites or toothpicks."

Roan's wife smacked her flyswatter against the arm of her yard chair.

"Penned. Like us. To be gawked at—just hanging on like a pus pocket under a toenail."

**

"I got to talk to yeu, Roan."

"Whert do yeu want?" he asked his wife when she came from the house dragging a quilt to the chair.

"Grandpa wants to be cremated." She sat down.

"What?"

"Cremated. His body—"

"I know what cremation means," Roan interrupted. "Did he lose his mind? No! An Indian is nert cremated. What in the shelf of beans did he mean? Anything but that. Drop him into the farmpond. Stake him to a tree. Put him in the earth. But not cremation! I won't do it."

"It's not up to you, Roan," his wife exerted. "Yeur sister, Weazel, is driving him down."

"When?"

"They're here now."

"Yeu just now knowd he was coming?"

"Nearly." Roan's wife looked at the thimble on her finger. "I might have knowd it a day or two ago. I can't be sure."

"Ner, yeu can't be sure if yeu don't want to be."

"See who comes into the backyard," Roan's wife said to Roan, looking up from the quilt she gathered close to her chair.

A wobbly old Indian man on a cane & a woman about the age of Roan got out of a Nash Rambler & walked into the backyard.

"I can't imagine who—" Roan looked over his shoulder. "Well, it's dad. How yeu be, sir?"

"I been getting along." The old man waddled into the circle of yard chairs. "This is the first time I seen the yard empty of all yeur boys sitting here like the earth was made up of nothing but Sundays."

Roan's wife tightened her threads, nearly pulling the coyote's hind legs up to his tail.

"Yerp. We do a lot of conflabing."

"Yer, we do." Roan's wife bit into the threads.

"I been thinking about my funeral," The old man said.

"Yeu knowd when it is?" Roan asked with alarm.

"Nowd. Nert exactly. But when it curms I dern't want yeu all standing around gawking at my box." Grandpa was sputtering as he talked. The spittle rested on his shirt front.

"This is wherd I gert t' listen to all day," Weazel, Roan's sister, moaned.

"He gets right to the business, don't he?" Roan looked at his sister & then his wife. "No how are yeu's, nice day, etc.— He just gets right into it."

Roan's wife listened to the old man as she worked with the coyote's puckered rump.

"I know my time is coming. I can feel it when I get up in the morning. I can feel it in my chair in the afternoons. At night, it's like a friend that I'm going to leave with soon. & right now, we're just sitting here talking about it—about the particulars of it, yeu understand."

"Yer, I do," Roan assured his father.

Weazel sobbed to think of her father leaving her alone on the place, though she could see Roan's house from hers. She sucked the runny tears back up her nose.

Roan's wife pulled her coyote quilt closer to her. "Which chair is death sitting in now, since it's always with yeu."

"It's right here with me, woman. It's me next on the trail." The old man snappered at her. "It's not goint to get mixed up as to which one it's taken next. It's ME!" He stomped his cane on the ground.

Roan's sister moved her foot.

"& I'm leaving here by cremation."

"Yeu're not!" Roan said. "It's an abomination for an Indian—"

"No, son. I've been thinking about it. It makes more sense to me than the other wayd of being pud in the earth & ground to chili powder by ther wurms."

"Father—" Roan's sister howled—

"When it's yeur time, yeu can say whad yeu think about it." He pounded his cane on the ground again.

"Why cremation?" Roan asked his father.

"There's something strange now—some reason I got to do it this way—It seems natural. It's like the way the earth is goint. & I'm standing in for it. I know we hain't done it before— My father was buried. His father was struck by an axe & was mourned on the death rack."

"Then he was buried."

"Yes, because the white man was having his way by that time & didn't want any dead Indians in the air." Roan's wife pulled at the rectum of the coyote until she got the threads loosened.

"I look around & see cremation. That's what I want done to my body."

**

She was probably the prettiest girl he had seen, & sweet. Kollar asked her to the chicken dance they did in spring rounds. Her black eyes shined & her black hair. Her skin seemed wet as morning dew when they finished the dance. He wanted to talk to her then. He wanted more than that. He wanted to get right on her, pull up her skirt & relieve his throbbing. The full force of his ache let go in her.

She was soft as rabbit fur. Sometimes he touched her arm. He thought he would have to have her. He asked his father.

"Yeu mean marriage?" Roan inquired as they sat in the backyard another afternoon with the fields spawning over the prairie to the several 100 feet of the Wichita Mountains far away.

"Yes," Kollar choked.

There was no other way he could have her. She would not let him do anything to her in the hay or the barn. She would be his for keeps. That's the way it was sometimes. He remembered when Gerp met his wife.

"Then talk to her father. It nert up to me," Roan said. "Tell him yeu want her for a wife. See what can be arranged. Yeu are old enough. I surpose she is."

"We'll give you a feast," Jake said. "Hang yeu in effage because yeu is gone from us as husband of that sweet chicken dancer. Whee bou tay."

"Yep. Yehu he gouth," his mother jobbered.

She would finally be his & his thing would not have rest for nights. It had wanted to rub in her since he first saw her. An arrow standing out from his groin.

Her father agreed to let her be married. But she thought about it. Kollar was nearly crazed while she took her time. She didn't want her girlhood to be over. She felt it had hardly started & then to be so quickly gone & she would be a wife & mother, she supposed. It was usually what happened. & she'd just been a child herself.

But Kollar told her she would still have her friends &
it would not be unpleasant.

Then why did she hear the women cry in church or
when they were in bed alone at night? she asked Kollar.

"Who," he asked impatiently, dismayed that any woman
would cry over being married to a man.

"Aunts. Cousins who come to visit now & then. Even my
own mother."

"Naw," Kollar said. "That happy little woman?"

"She cries worse them them all. It's a fact," she told him.

"Yeu won't cry."

"Yes I will," She said & spoke no other word for several
days.

He thought she must be ample under her skirt. He
wanted his mouth on her & his hard thing in her. No, she
wouldn't cry.

He kissed her after another chicken dance & she said
she would marry him. He stroked her cheek. She moaned
& he thought she must feel the passion for him too. She
smiled at him. Her skin was dewy & wet again. He could
hardly withdraw himself from her, turn away & tell Roan
& his mother, Grandpa & Weazel & the others, she was
going to be his wife.

She smiled at him the same way at the wedding. They
made their vows, kissed & ate the feast. He took her away
in his Citation with the sunroof up to a room he rented for
the night. He kissed her again, touched her body softly,
holding himself back so as not to scare her. He put her on
the bed & climbed onto her & she made a way for him. He
sank into her. He could tell by her breath that she felt no
pleasure with his passage into her. He would make it better

for her later, but for now he pumped & pumped & finally
released his ache.

**

It was a rainy autumn day. Splots of dust on the
windows turned to mud. Trees hissed.

The pond, flat & wide & shallow as Jake, had foamed
when they passed it on the county road. Mud-splots pelted
Roan's 20-year-old Plymouth in the drive. His wife sat in
the room with the quilt she was working on.

"Yer. The earth could fly off—" Roan sermoned them.
Gerp's small children had their noses pushed to the door
because they couldn't go out in the rain.

"Ah, led them—" Kollar said.

"Naw. Their mother'd ged on me when I ged back. She'd
be the one to clean mud oud of their ears."

A gust of wind stroked the house.

"Yeu should see the white caps on the flat farm pond,
Roan—6 footers when we passed. Yerp. Bruted in the
leaves," Jake said.

"It's a day we have to hold on." Roan shook his head.
"This might be one of those goint there days."

"I think you got the buffalo before the spear," Gerp said.
"We ain't going nowhere. The country is sturdy as Jake's
rump on the chair in yeur yard. Been waiting for him to
leave for years, but he nert goint to. I don't blame him. I'd
be sittin there fer good too. The cookin, the room to stay in
when it gets too hard. Well, he knows what he's doing. & the
earth does too. Yeu can be sure. It's goint to be here long
after us. Now all this talk of our end being eminent is hog
gauls. We being only a mumbly peg in the Great Spirit's

hand. & Roan & ma praying every day to preserve us, God, keep us in this land we had ripped off from us once that we're hanging on to now only by our hang nails. Yeu can't do it again to us, God. We just put in a row of beans. Don't let that 'ere bomb blow us to Tucumcari or even farther into outer space. The hunting grounds, pleasant as they be for us, ain't quite ready for 'em yet. Just let us get in one more crop on grandpa's field & God bless the hungry people of the world. Take them, Great Father, not us yet, who still have to get what we're trying to from the land. Let our little ones grow up. It can't be asking too much."

"Just a while longer, Jesus," Kollar said.

"Jars cause he got a new wife now he wand to be screwing into," Jake interrupted.

"Watch yeurself, boy," Kollar warned.

"I ain't believing we're goint no more than 6 footers on the pond," Gerp said. "Could be maybe Jake or some other whale in it, but I can't believe no wind would do that. Yeu think I believe anything just cause I'm stupid. No. I dern't."

"Well then get yeur rump off the chair & earn a living or stand in a picket line or chase hogs or due SOME-THING," his mother said.

Roan looked at his wife to see where she was from. She was always half dead sewing in her chair, up to her nose in scraps of material & sacks of who-knows-what surrounding her, not paying much attention to the boys or even old Roan himself, then she'd be in the middle driving them like bulls out to pasture. It was consistency they lacked. Most of them. Yeu'd think they were the nicest boys, then yeu'd see one of them ripping out old ladies' hairnets at the dime store or peeing on the street, & yeu'd know their manners

were veneer—the deal bureau in the shed with its top all
curled up from the weather. Well, things aren't always as
they seem.

"How's Grandpa?" Gerp asked.

"Still breathin'," Roan answered.

"Iz he up to seeing the kids terday? I thoud we might go
up there in the rain if he be feeling—"

"If yeu wand to hear how he wantz t' be cremated,"
Kollar said.

"Iz he still on thad one?" Gerp asked. "I was thinking we
could move in with Aunt Weazel after—"

"Yeu take that up with Weazel."

"I thought yeu could put in a wurd for me. She'll need
help keeping the place up—"

"He hain't gone yed," Kollar grumped as though he
were thinking of moving there himself.

"How's yeur wife?" Gerp thought to ask him.

"She fine. Working today. She's spooked by that coyote
witch woman quilt you gave us, ma," Kollar said. "I'm
thinking about giving it back to yeu for Jake or Gerp's wife
or children."

"Whad about it scirs her?"

"I don't know. She keeps it in the closet unless she
knows yeu & Roan are coming."

"Well, I'll make her a new one then. Can't look too
peaceful though, the night spirits be camping out on it."

"I told her that, but she says she feels it brings the
spirits."

"Dars," Jake said. "& everybody telling me to get a
wife?"

"We're going to go cold this winter unless yeu get us another one made, ma."

"All right," she sneered. "This coyote one?"

"Ner, not that one either."

She sat with her grandchildren on her lap trying to sew. She whipped a striped yard on the floor of the coyote quilt. A fish swimming upstream on its side. She made a border of stars & trees like horns in the background.

"Can't yeu clear oud some of thad brush—" Kollar asked.

She sighed & looked at him as the wind wiped over the house again.

**

"We'll get anuther quilt," Kollar said on the edge of the bed. "Ma said so terday."

"Whad yeu tell her?"

"Wal, we were sittin' at Roan's talking about something & I jus sed that yeu didn't like the witch woman quilt."

"Naw! She'd get mad!" Kollar's wife lifted from the pillow.

"She'll be making us another one." Kollar put his hand on his wife & opened the neck of her nightgown. He kissed her cheek & neck. She moaned & he got under the covers with her. "Whad kind of quilt do yeu want?"

"I thought maybe some flower baskets."

"Ars," Kollar said. "Like these little flowers here on yeur nightgown?" He unbuttoned her gown farther & kissed her bare shoulder. "Like these little flower baskets?" He kissed her breasts.

"Kollar," she moaned.

"Whad yeu want?"

"I want yeu to keep kissing me."

"Ar, yeu do?" He kissed her mouth. "Yeu'll have to keep asking for id, then." Kollar said in her ear. "I durnt knowd if I'm in the mood."

"Touch me," she said.

"Whar?" he asked.

"On my ear."

He kissed her ear.

"On my neck."

He kissed her neck again.

"My shoulder."

Kollar kept kissing his wife. "Yeu smell like soap." He said. "Clean as sunshine. Clean as the farm pond." He kissed her navel. "Clean as the little flower baskets yeu want."

"Kollar," his wife said. "I like for yeu to touch me."

"Yeu wand me ter keep doing id?"

"Yes," she whispered. "Yes, Kollar."

"Wherd yeu want now?" he asked, hoping it wouldn't take her too long because he was stiff as the handle of the garden hoe.

"My legs."

Kollar kissed her thighs, & behind her knees. He kissed her ankle & knew he was already leaking out of himself. He took his hand back up her thigh & spread her legs. He found her passage & put his finger into it. She was wet for him. He could wait no longer. He got on her & thrust himself into her. She moaned & held onto him. He rode her for his own pleasure & felt her moving under him. She wanted him.

She wanted him, for the first time, he knew she was with
him. He kissed her, held off as long as he could, but finally
pumped his seed out, & she, the dark garden soil, received
his single-blade plow.

**

"This 'ere's a moveable earth." Roan said in his chair by
the window. "Like a jigsaw puzzle someone's trying to put
together. One part of the north is in the wrong place here.
Blizzard-wind too early in my yard in Oklahoma. Just look
at 'er blow."

Kollar & his wife stood near the window by Roan.
They'd come for a supper & a visit.

Roan's wife kicked the lid of the wood stove closed. Near
it, a few rocks held down the warped place in the linoleum.
Around the room were stacks of her attempts at quilt-
making. Sacks & sacks of material she had saved from
everything they ever wore. Other projects were wedged
between pieces of heavy furniture. She left dishes & condi-
ments from her cooking on the cabinet. There was hardly
a place to step in the house. Even the walls were crowded
with her work. She had sewn Christ rising from the smoke
of a sweat lodge fire. She had pieced cormorants from quilt
scraps. Roan looked at them & sat with his feet on the
rabbit cage he had brought in from the yard. One day he
would finish it for Gerp's children.

"Maybe the Great Spirit set this weather in just to see
how it looked."

Roan's wife stared at him. "Wherd yeu suppose our
weather is—?"

"Probably up in the north pole where this weather came from. Give him a day or so. He'll get it straightened out." Roan shucked the paper from his lap, stared into the wind that danced the autumn leaves like steam hissing from his sweat lodge rocks. Soon he got up, but not until the phone rang.

His sister called about his father.

"Grandpa says the white buffalo is in the field. Do you see anything?" Weazel asked.

Roan went to the window. "Naw," he returned to the phone. "Tell him it's his imagination."

"I did," his sister answered. "He said everything is imagination."

"Let me talk to him."

"I don't think he can get out of bed," Weazel said.

"He was standing at the window gawking at the starm-wind, wasn't he?"

"Yes, but I got him back into bed. He's under his buffalo robe," Weazel reported. "'There's no starm,' he says. 'Just the wind.'"

"How's he seeing into the weather anywayd? He's not been seeing anything too well for a while."

"He's got Gerp's binoculars. The ones he buyed his kids to see the stars."

"Whodever thought yeu could see the sters up close until yeu got there— This is a moveable universe."

"Well, it was in them he got the sight of his white buffalo."

"When does he want his funeral?"

"It's his cremation he's been talking about."

"That's been decided, sister! I finished that business when he was here on my place."

"Maybe yeu finished it, but he didn't."

"I won't have my father cremated. He's not dead yet anyway," Roan shouted. "If he doesn't shud up, I'm going to arrange his cremation before he is!"

"HArrmmm," Roan's wife cleared her throat.

"Get the old man out of bed. Whad else did yeu call for?"

"Do yeu want him with yeu?" Weazel asked.

"Maybe I could talk to him if he was."

"I'll bring him over anytime."

"In the blizzard?" Roan said.

"In a volcano if there be one." Weazel put her hand over the phone. Roan could hear her muffled call to their father. "Well, he's not coming," she told Roan.

"What did you call for then?"

"To tell you he couldn't talk," she answered her brother. "To tell yeu that he seen the white buffalo he says is standing in the field. & to tell yeu his end is coming—is what he says there in bed."

Roan looked at his wife impatiently. "Do yeu want to talk to the sister?"

"Ner," she said presently. "I'm snibbing these threads between stirring the meat."

"Jes like the Great Spirit hisself—" Roan preached to the air, "snibbing out parts of the earth, setting em down & letting his angels move them around just for their boredom on these days."

Roan's wife scratched her side with the scissors & looked over the scraps for the quilt.

"Gurs. Just tell him I hain't seen no white buffalo today, ner any day, for thad matter. & I sure don't see no funeral pire flaring up over the earth for him."

"Well, he do," she said & hung up the phone.

"I'm thinking of an unlisted number," Roan sat back down in his chair at the window. Kollar & his wife were piled together on the sofa. Roan's wife whittled at the supper for a while, then sat down with the new quilt she worked on for Kollar & his wife. A razor-back deer with horns that made a woodland on its head. 2 rodents in the corner.

"Creation & Cremation," She said.

Kollar's wife looked at her mother-in-law.

The moon with an eye. & a missile with snake's skin crawling through the clouds.

"I was thinking of a flowers-in-the-field pattern, or Jacob's-ladder." The new wife had gumption.

Roan hit his shoe.

"Whad yeu think this iz?" Roan's wife sneered. "Id's a Jacob's-ladder if ever I seen one. What yeu think is coming down now?" She looked at the girl with her tooth open.

Kollar still slobbered over her.

**

Gerp was drinking in the sky in Roan's backyard like turpentine.

"Yeu been hearing how the earth's goint ter come apard," Jake said. "What do yeu think?"

"I durn't know." Gerp looked at Jake for the first time.

"Yeu don't know anything."

Gerp looked back to the sky. His kids running around the rabbit cage Roan finished for them. Jake's dogs barking. "I think it nert anything. We're going to be here forever like we always been. We are. Just yeu watch."

"I plan to," Jake said. "But it's him always talking about the end that's jermping in my socks like ants. He's always got ter talk about the end," Jake surped. "Just like it were coming."

"Yerp."

"& it is," Roan came to sit with his boys.

"Whad yeu mean, pa?"

"Whad end is id this time? The end of the day or the end of us staying in yeur yard?"

"The end of us living on the earth."

"Well, I don'd know if I wand to talk about that again."

"I do, & I want to tell yeu, in case I hain't here sometime when yeu come. I don't want yeu to get scired. I want yeu to hang on cause yeu goint to be all right, even though yeu won't think so for a while."

"What makes yeu think we won't be goint with yeu, pa, if we be goint at all?"

"Because yeu might not believe enough to be lifted out of here on the first wave that's goint. I'm looking for it, boys, I believe it's coming. So does yeur mother. We don't want to leave any of yeu, but we know we're going first. Maybe it will take the rest of yeu longer. There'll be war & then some peace & then things will get bad again. Different ones of us will leave at different times—there will be different ranks in eternity, yeu see. Some will go before the war, some after—some during the peace before it gets bad again. Then others won't go until it's all over. That's why there's so much argument over the goint time, because there's not just one time of exit."

"Yaar." Jake had his finger in his ear.

Gerp looked at a hole in the yard tree.

"Then we'll all be together again in a land that's still on the far horizon. Getting closer all the time though. Don't worry none. It's coming sure as if it were already here."

"I hain't doubted yeu before, pa. I don't want to stay here if yeu aren't," Gerp said. "But I can't just see it yet."

"Then just believe the end is coming, & there won't be nothing left here that yeu want to live for anyway. The Great Spirit takes us from the earth before we get hurt, believe that & yeu'll be goint too."

"How?" Jake asked with his hand raised.

"I can't exactly tell you, Jake, other than that we just be lifted off the earth into the sky."

"Naw."

"Yerp. I'm waiting like the little grandkids coming around saying pick me up."

"Gwarny," Jake said.

"It's like God cutting his toenails, different parts go at different times," Roan tried to make himself clear to his sons. "Beginning. Middle. End. Just like waves of the removal of our 5 Civilized Tribes to Indian Territory."

Gerp hit his jaw.

"Truly son, I think yeu understand."

"He don't know nothing." Jake told his father. "He'll be sitting here looking at the sky when we already been up there fer years. But I know whad yeu mean."

Roan rubbed his overalls.

**

Now it was 2 white tornadoes coming out of a black sky where Roan's wife sat in the Indian summer. The funnels became horns of a large, square antelope. 4 branching trees made its legs. A striped horse blanket fell like a road from the distance for its tail.

Grandpa coughed all over the yard, the binoculars still around his neck. Weazel brought him over but he got himself bent double & Jake & Roan nearly had to pull him in 2 to get him straightened in the yard chair again. Then they worked another hour getting him back to his house in Weazel's Nash Rambler.

"Whad will I du wid the witch quilt that Kollar & his new wife dond wand?" Roan's wife asked when Grandpa was tucked away in his bed & Roan & Jake were back to sitting in their yard chairs.

"Grandpa could use another blanket on him," Roan said. "The older he gets, the colder he is all the time."

"Hardly nothing going to keep him warm anymore." Jake sneered his words.

"He nert been too good. We barely got him home."

"He'll be kicking a long time," Jake said.

"Naw, he won't, Jake. I heard the death chant in him. Sitting right there in that yard chair."

Roan's wife moved.

Jake looked kind of peaked for a minute.

"Hain't left no death boogers on it for yeu," Gerp said, coming into the yard.

"Snerd," Jake said to his brother & jumped out of his

yard chair, throwing Gerp to the ground. Gerp screamed & thrashed.

"Gaulbation," Roan sammered. "Quit that ruckus!"

"Both of them could go for all I'm concerned," Their mother said.

"When yeu querts hain't here, which is never, yeur ma & I sit peaceable."

"Yeu always got an anecdote for us, pa," Jake said. "What would yeu talk about without us here to fuss about?"

Roan's sister had been calling his name from her house. They'd been hearing it, but nobody paid any attention for a moment.

"Roan!" Her stringy voice persisted. Finally at her tremolo, Roan looked over his shoulder.

"How long yeu goint to let her beller?"

"Til she gets hauze."

"OOooOOooOOooOOooOOooOOoo."

"She's not goint to let up," Roan's wife told him.

"Maybe it's about grandpa." Gerp worried.

"Hain't seen his spirit flying over yet," Roan's wife looked up.

"Maybe he went the other way."

Roan picked up the dog's dish by his chair & threw it at Jake's head.

"WAOOU." Jake held his forehead where a lump soon jumped.

"Go see whad yeur aunt wants," Roan told Jake.

"Soon as I don't see the scum floating around in my head." Jake still winced from the pain.

"I'll go, Roan," Gerp said. "I came out to see grandpa anywayd."

Gerp jumped up from his yard chair & ran across the stubbled field between the 2 small houses.

When Roan's sister saw her nephew coming, she jumped up & down on the backstairs. "Roan. Roan," she screamed.

"Is it grandpa?" Gerp asked.

"Who else do yeu think lives here?" Weazel snapped.

"Pa," Gerp screamed before he got out of the field.

Roan looked at him.

"I think it might be about grandpa," Roan's wife told him.

"Yes sur, it du." Roan got up out of his chair. Jake's dog barked. An old hound that lived under a stoop to the shed began to howl. "Ah, shubber!" Roan told him with a flap of his arm & the hound crawled back to his shelter.

"Whizzend wrong?" Roan asked as he met Gerp at the edge of the field.

"I dunno. She just said for yeu to come. It's grandpa but I don't know how bad."

"He's bad dead," Jake said, who followed his father a little wobbly. "That turquoise fibber is twittering at yeur side."

"I'll come with yeu," Kollar arrived at Roan's then too & the men started through the field.

**

Grandpa was dead. There was no doubt about it. His eyes looked straight to the ceiling where his spirit had just passed.

Outside, the dogs still howled, even the one always licking his rear.

"I was doing the dishes, just soon as we got him back in his bed," Roan's sister said. "Not paying attention to anything. & when I stopped running water, I heard his death chant again. He's been doing it every day for a long time now."

"I knowd. I heard it."

"But when I got upstairs, it was kind of a moan." Roan's sister put her head in her hands & sobbed. Roan took Weazel against his chest. "He kept lifting his hands toward the ceiling & finally he couldn't lift them anymore & they fell at his side. I heard his last breath go out of him just like air out of a car tire. His eyes stopped looking & his mouth stayed open a little."

Roan tried to close his father's mouth, but it wouldn't close. It just sagged back open several times & Roan gave up.

"Let him catch the flies now," Jake said.

Roan thought of hitting Jake on the black place on the side of his face again, but didn't. "Get yeur ma," Roan said to Kollar. "Tell her to bring the witch quilt. I knowd whad she can do with it now."

Kollar stumbled backward out of his grandpa's room, staring at the dead body a moment longer.

"Kollar," Roan said & he backed hurriedly from the room.

"He looks like he's still breathing." Weazel stared at her father.

"It's all right. He's dead," Roan told his sister. "He knew it was coming. I think he was ready to go back to the spirit."

At that, the old man let out a shudder & the sister screamed. Jake nearly jumped out of his Oklahoma carp sweatshirt.

"Woah," Roan touched the old man. "There now." He stood holding the shoulders of the dead man.

Roan's sister, horrified, watched them.

"Is he coming back, pa?" Jake stuttered.

They stood over him a moment.

"Naw, he's dead." Roan assured him after a moment. "It's just some reaction or reflex." Roan had his ear on his father's chest. Then he put his ear to his nose & listened for a long time. "There's no breath. If he was coming back, he changed his mind. He's gone."

The three of them stood over the old man until Kollar & his mother came into the room. They heard them climb the stairs like a tribe of ghosts themselves.

"Where'd that little fart go that's always hanging around?" Roan asked without turning.

"I haint seen him since yeu stood up in the yard."

Roan's wife looked at her father-in-law when she came in the room with the witch quilt. "Grandpa," she said tenderly & touched the old man's arm.

"Watch oud," Jake said. "He been backfiring."

She looked at her son.

"He supped a moment ago in the room as though taking in one more breath." Roan said. "It eazered back out though. I heard every bit of it. There haint no air left in thar now."

Roan took his wife in his arm to comfort her. Kollar & his aunt stood near them. Jake still stared at the old man.

"Close yeur mouth, Jake," his mother told him. "One agape is enough."

Jake stood straight by the foot of the bed then.

Roan lead the small family group in prayer.

"Hey ye ye ye. Hey ye ye ye." They chanted until the peace that passed understanding limped over them as though it were a dog without a hind leg.

Roan's wife pulled the witch quilt over him. "I got to make another one to bury him," She said.

**

Grandpa's body lay in his bed for another day. "Well, we're goint to have to do something wid him," Roan's wife said.

"We're going to have to bury him," Gerp said when he came the next morning.

"I been thinking that too," Roan told him. "I'll find the minister & we'll see about his burying."

Roan's wife was afire cutting out stripes of bright yellow & blue cloth on her breadboard. She was going to make a burying quilt for grandpa. She had Gerp's wife helping her & Kollar's. They sat wherever they could find a place among the piles of boxes & sacks & heavy furniture that filled the room. Weazel had stayed up late into the night with her sister-in-law. Gerp's kids running wild all over the place until Roan made Gerp take them home. Kollar's baby wasn't coming up for a while yet.

"& I don't want one of them quilts for him neither," she had already told Kollar.

Roan's wife had a pattern in mind. A cornfield of blue & yellow stripes, bright as the sun shining on the field between the houses. A straight road & the narrow house grandpa lived in with his daughter. & over the house & fields, a shadow of something. A bird or hawk?

"I need some black cloth. Something special," she said. "I durno jes whad this shadow iz," Roan's wife confided in him. "Bud it up there. I knowd that."

"Whar's his white buffalo?" Roan asked her. He was going to gather the old man's pipe & wool pants & moccasins to dress him in.

"What's that hammering over at the sister's?" Kollar's wife asked as she stitched a blue & yellow stripe together for a cornfield.

"That's my sister hammering a death rack. But he hain't goint to stay there long. We got laws now to bury a man."

Roan asked Gerp's wife if he could have the binoculars. Grandpa had died with them in his hands. He'd also asked for a magnifying glass. "I guers it's all right," she said, sewing the corner of the house to the straight road on the coffin-shaped quilt.

"We'll have this finished by sundown."

"Id be quicker to use my machine," Gerp's wife said.

"No machine is goint to touch my hand-stitched quilts. It's like artificial insimination of the heifer."

Kollar's wife laughed.

Roan's wife stopped long enough to make lunch for them. When Weazel came in the door, she looked hungry as they were.

"Jake," she said. "I need you to get off yeur tail & help me with grandpa's death rack."

"Sure," Jake told her. "One of my favorite things to do."

"Whad kind of quilt yeu making?" Roan's sister asked the wife.

"Jes a cornfield & yeur house & road."

Kollar's wife got up from the table & held it up for Roan's sister to see.

"Now that a bright, pretty quilt. Grandpa would like that. Whad those holes still in it?" she asked.

"I'm making a shadow of some kind over the field. I dunnod yet what it iz." Roan's wife pulled at her mouth. "I'm goint to need some black cloth & I hain't got any. I use it more than any other— Maybe I'll send Kollar to the store in Lawton this afternoon. I need it quick now."

Weazel finished up the dishes while the women got to work on the quilt again. A little blue spit of a door in the house. Two windows like navels.

The men worked on the death rack. The minister & another man, a county official, talked as they hammered.

Roan's sister rushed in the back door just as Roan's wife was going to call Jake or Roan to go to the yard-goods for her.

"I found this piece-goods in the shed." She handed the black cloth to Roan's wife.

She put it to her nose. "It god a jabbered smell— kerosene?"

"It's the black cloth yeu need. I can't spare any men."

"Yeu get the death papers signed?" Roan's wife asked Weazel as she left.

"Yip."

Roan's wife continued to inspect it. "I guers it all right. Save the men a trip. We don't have much longer, girls, to get this finished. Grandpa's goint to get as ripe as this quilt if we don't get moving."

Roan's wife cut out some spindly shapes of the black cloth. Rubbed them with a stone until they looked worn & feathery. "Jes like a hawk wing." She said, and pieced it to the quilt. Now she had to work on the quilt alone. The girls had done all they could. It was nearly done. They got up & stretched their backs & moaned.

"Maybe it were a flying buffalo Grandpa saw wid the binoculars." She puzzled. "It's a strange critter rising over Grandpa's cornfields."

The girls stood around her until she shushed them off. "I can't work being watched at," she complained.

"There ain't really no place else to go in this crowded house." Kollar's wife looked at the piecings of cormorants on the wall.

They left to look at the death rack in grandpa's yard. The men sweated in the warm fall afternoon as they worked. Finally Gerp & his wife gathered up their children & went home.

Jake tested the strength of the rack by jumping up & down on it. Kollar got to laughing so hard his wife heard him clear from inside the house where she'd gone to help bathe grandpa.

"Pregnant women shouldn't be washing the dead," Roan's sister told her.

Yes, she could, she said. She was praying for the wisdom of the old man to pass into the child she carried.

Somehow it was after dark when they got grandpa fixed up on the death rack. They had wrapped him in the quilt

Roan's wife finished. His trinkets were in his hand & his hair braided.

After dinner they went back in Roan's sister's house & lit some cedar. The friends came to the yard, a few of them. They talked in honor of him, & made prayer chants for grandpa's journey to the happy hunting grounds with Chief Christ. He was on his way now. They looked up into the stars through the tree. Then they would bury him in the Indian cemetery the next afternoon.

**

In the morning sun, Roan saw something strange from his window. The death rack smoked. "Whad—" he asked.

Roan's wife looked from the window too. "He's on far," she said.

Roan got his pants on & ran out of the house through the cornfield. Already the little flames leaped over him. Roan banged on his sister's back door. She didn't come too quick either. "Whad yeu want?"

"Look at grandpa."

The sister screamed when she saw the death rack on fire.

"Where's yeur hose?"

"In the shed."

Roan ran to the old shed & ripped off the door. He fumbled through his sister's belongings. Rake. Hoes. Cultivator blades. Finally the hose.

He ran back to the house.

"The outside water's turned off," Roan's sister told him in her robe. "Yeu'll have to gert under the house to turn it on. I got the opening boarded up so the animals won't hibernate there in winter."

"Run some kettles of water."

"No, Roan," she said. "It's too late. You couldn't throw a kettle of water that high anyway. The step ladder against it would topple it." She began crying. "Grandpa. Dad. It's what he wanted, Roan." She whimpered, running around the yard. "Yeu know that."

"How did it happen?" Roan asked, looking now at the death rack which was blazing under smoke.

"I wiped the kerosene lantern with the black cloth I gave yeur wife to make the shadow on the quilt." Weazel looked at Roan. "Then last night I thought he might want some matches for his pipe, so I put them in his hand. Just under the binoculars. When the marning sun came up—I figured if he was surposed to go up—"

"All right, woman," Roan said. "Yeu & grandpa have yeur way."

"Yar, he fried like a hot dog," Jake said, "flubbering in grease up there on the death rack."

**

Roan sat depressed in his house for the next month as autumn slowly licked the yard & edges of the farm. The charred place in the back of Weazel's depressed him even more when he saw it.

"Whad the old man want cremated for?" Roan asked his wife. "He was set on it."

"Just the way the world might go," she guessed. Otherwise, Roan's wife didn't know. "But that 'ere black on his death quilt were the smoke of his cremation. It were surposed to be."

**

Before the dark went down, Roan began the rock pile for the sweat lodge. He took the rocks from the pit one by one & carried them back to the bare place in the yard where he always built his fire. The turquoise ghost jumped around him. "My pet," Roan moaned to it. Other spirits in the pack that camped on his land gathered around the rock pile.

Gerp, Kollar, & Jake spread the hides over the frame of the sweat lodge & tied them in place. It made a round hump in the backyard, about the height of a man.

Roan's wife sat like a mortuary stone nearby.

Before dawn Roan would start the fire & hear the voices of his ancestors again.

Yellowed clouds stuffed the cracks in the sky as Roan carried logs for the fire. "It's more than just pond scum we're living under," he told his boys. "From the far east & south, the spirits gather for strength to take back to their part."

A heaviness sat upon Jake. For some reason he was not in the mood for the intense heat in the sweat lodge at dawn. It was a test of endurance to sit through the 4 rounds, each hotter than the last. It cleansed the body of toxins & made the spirit strong.

"Garnation," Jake murmured.

Roan made sure his boys attended.

**

In the dark before dawn, Roan's family stood around the rock pile as Roan lit the logs with some papers. A fire rose in the darkness. Dogs howled in the distance. The children shivered & whimpered by their mother until she & Gerp held them. Kollar's wife, big as a sow, would not go into the sweat lodge because of her condition. The brothers talked as the fire stood in the yard & began heating the rocks.

The women sat in the yard chairs they drew near. The heat warmed their faces, stung their toes. Soon they moved back from the fire.

After a while, the dawn began to show. A basket of sage & medicine herbs was passed. The women & children stood around the fire now with the men. Everyone grew quiet.

Roan stood at the head of the fire by the red cow skull on a post. "Father, we're grateful for the ordonnace of yeur hand on our pants saying this way, not that. Yeu blow up this tight ball we live on, bring us up inter the heavenlies. Holy Father, Lamb of God. Yeu ride with us to the end. We coming to poverty & hardship & not having supper on the table when it should be there. These spirits from poor countries go back with strength. Turn the dipper out for them. None of us deserving, yet yeu provide."

When Roan finished his prayer, he stood silent for a moment with his arms raised. Then they each had a turn at the head of the fire by the red cow skull. They held the sage & herbs in their hand, stood facing the Great Spirit with some unspoken request in their heads.

Afterwards, they entered the sweat lodge. The men first, then the women & children, bending to enter the door, they formed a circle around the empty pit, drawing up their legs in the cramped sweat lodge.

Roan had elected Kollar to carry the heated rocks on a pitchfork to the pit in the sweat lodge, & to stay outside during the ceremony to close & open the flap of the tent.

They sat in silence for a while. Soon Kollar brought in a rock from the fire & then several others. Roan sprinkled them with water from a bucket. Chanted a prayer & raised several totems before them.

Kollar closed the flap of the sweat lodge.

In the dark, Gerp's children complained because of the heat that began to stir in the lodge.

"Bless Weazel," Roan began his prayers. "Yank the sorrow of missing grandpa from her. We don't sorrow as others—we got the hunting grounds to look forward to. Bless Kollar's wife & baby soon to come. If time weren't out of whack, he'd be here already. Bless Gerp's children & wife. Jake—well, bless him too. My wife. Her quilts." Roan prayed for the Indian people—that they keep strong & remember their ways. He prayed for the leaders of the world. He prayed for the poor & sick.

Then he was quiet & the others had a chance for their petitions.

"Yar—I see grandpa up thar homesteading space," Roan's wife simmered. "Laying out his claim on a piece of that far sky—according to how he lived his life."

Weazel wept at the thought of her father.

Gerp prayed for another place to live, hoping Weazel would hear & remember his prayer when she was alone in the house.

Each of them asked what they wanted of the Great Spirit. The heat made sweat run down their faces, though no one could see it in the blackness. It was a welcome dark in the sweat lodge before the mean red glow of the rocks in the pit.

When Kollar lifted the flap of the sweat lodge, the cool morning air & the new light rushed into them. Roan took a drink of water from the bucket. Then he passed the dipper. The children left the lodge. They only stayed one round.

Kollar brought more rocks from the fire. They hissed & spit when he put them in the pit. Then he closed the flap & the heat climbed over them. Roan sprinkled the rocks with water from the bucket. They chanted in their rock language & Roan chanted.

"I have vision of the earth with a cloud hanging over it," Roan said presently— "Just like that quilt yeu made grandpa," he said to his wife. "I see the bluestem & blackjack. The sumac groves along the cotton fields. The elder & lindens all the way to the Wichita Mountains. There's cars galloping on the highway—& up high over the sky, up in the universe, there's grandpa on his piece of the happy hunting ground—smiling like a red-tailed hawk I see sometimes in the tree. Yer, he decided to be a sign of the earth."

Roan's sister moaned again when he said this.

"He's got his burial quilt around him, the binoculars at his neck. All around him the red haze of the fire.

"Hitch ack ay ay. He says—

"Hey yey.

"Hitch. Tch."

The others joined his chanting as the holy sweat lodge filled with heat & sound, pushing them over the edge of the earth, out into the vast universe where they had come from, where they were going again. Weazel's soul longed for release as she hawed with the others.

Soon Kollar lifted the tent flap & the cool air rushed in. They drank from the dipper & sat in silence for some moments. Weazel longed for the flap to be closed again so she could be invisible in her grief. Kollar brought more rocks on the pitchfork. They were red with heat.

Weazel went outside for a short spell, then returned to her place on the other side of Roan's wife. She wiped her face. Gerp's wife left to stay with Kollar's wife & the children. The later rounds were too hot for her.

Kollar closed the flap & the 3rd round began with the grip of heat at their bodies. Any sore stung with heat. They cringed, squirmed in their places. The rocks hissed more fiercely this time when Roan struck them with water. The pit glowed at their feet. It was the hell they were saved from. They felt kay-os for a moment to appreciate the order they lived in.

"This earth is just a womb." Roan talked in the dark. "The circle of the womb in the universe where we grow & are taken out at death.

"I see the cinders dropping off grandpa. The flames no longer rising from his transparent body. Already the earth trembles. I hear the voices of our people struggling in their daily lives—some of them are falling, some rising—bless them, Great Spirit. I hear some of them stepping out of their own visions into Chief Christ's. I see the decisions being made. Otherwise it's a trigger dance we're doing.

"It's going to be like a wedding we're invited to—& right now we're getting lined up to be sucked up into heaven. The point is to seek the larger vision—thar's only one way, that of the Great Spirit through Christ our lord."

"Amen."

"Yey bote," Roan's sister moaned.

"Ke yoo," Jake said.

"E oo E oo." Weazel's tremolo was deafening for a moment.

"The Great Spirit pours out his baskets upon us to preserve us as long as he can. The anger of the world is building up. Mountains snorting their grief. Even the animals are groaning. We're fighting for our place in the hereafter. Be strong. Life is a sizable thing," Roan said.

"We got taken here on the back of the prairie, our land ripped out from underneath us like one of them tablecloths with our dishes left standing where they be. But we got to go on, live as though the land was ours. Nothing we can do. Our ways are gone until we get to the happy hunting grounds."

Roan talked while the terrible heat flew around the sweat lodge like bats. Weazel wondered why Kollar didn't open the flap. She knew it was time. Had something happened? She fought her panic. The sweat lodge brought her sorrow to the surface. She didn't want to let go of all of it yet.

"We're here on the edge scrambling for our place the size of a toenail."

Weazel wanted to bolt from her place, rip off the door-flap of the sweat lodge. Breathe something other than the stifling heat. Beat Kollar on the head for leaving her so long. She thought if she stood, she'd fall into the rock pit & be burned. A dark wave came over her but she lasted through it.

Soon, Kollar lifted the flap & relief rushed in with the cool air.

"Yeu took yeur time, sonny," she said to him as she wobbled from the lodge on trembling legs.

"I had to straighten out the kids that was fighting," he told her, "& Jake's dogs."

Weazel leaned against the post where the red cow skull hung. Soon the short rest was over & the 4th & last round began.

"I used to watch grandpa snerp tiddlywinks & chew jujubes," Roan said as they waited for Kollar to bring the last of the rocks to the pit of the sweat lodge. "That red Oklahoma mud on his moccasins. I used to think that was all there was to living."

Weazel felt crusted as grandpa's moccasins. Crusted as Roan's old Plymouth he drove down the dirt road until he could hardly see where he was going.

Kollar had all the rocks from the fire in the pit now. Weazel shrank until she was a rabbit with red eyes. Albino eyes. & the molten eye of the deer.

"Hayno," Roan said.

"God the whole earth iz goint erp," Weazel said, but the flap was closed now & the heat gripped her so intensely she screamed & choked & spit out the worst of her sorrow like it were a black, rotten walnut caught in her throat. "OOOOee ooooEEE."

For a moment in the last, short blast of heat, they were nothing more than a fireball on the prairie. They felt extinction pass over them like hogs when Roan steamed off their hairs. The air in the sweat lodge was brown. Then Kollar, paying attention this time, opened the flap & they crawled out.

"Webjubda. You had all of creation screeching with you, sister," Roan said.

Outside in the yard, the trees danced in the last of their moccasins. Yellows & ochres, the russet post oaks. Then sumac & maple. "The fall is red with heat as the rocks in the pit of the sweat lodge." Roan buckled his knee. "But id breaking up soon."

They ate some fruit & nuts in the yard after the sweat lodge ceremony & talked together. Weazel was feeling better.

"Reminds me of a game of tiddlywinks." Roan chuckled & looked off into the sky.

"What is it, Roan?" Gerp asked. "What does it look like from where yeu see?"

Roan, who never saw anything but the end he always said they were coming to, turned his hollow eye close to the sky & said it looked pretty much like this 'ere red autumn, f it were stuck somewhere in outer space.

"Cremation, Roan," his wife said.

TIME SHARE

Date: 12/7/17

TIME SHARE

Written by PATRICK KELLER
Illustrated and colored by DAN McDAID

Lettered by Crank!
Designed by Fred Chao

An Oni Press Publication

TIME SHARE
BY PATRICK KELLER & DAN MCDAID

Published by Oni Press, Inc.
Joe Nozemack, publisher
James Lucas Jones, editor in chief
David Dissanayake, sales manager
Andrew McIntire, v.p. of marketing & sales
Rachel Reed, publicity coordinator
Troy Look, director of design & production
Hilary Thompson, graphic designer
Angie Dobson, digital prepress technician
Ari Yarwood, managing editor
Charlie Chu, senior editor
Robin Herrera, editor
Bess Pallares, editorial assistant
Brad Rooks, director of logistics
Jung Lee, logistics associate

Oni Press, Inc
1305 SE Martin Luther King, Jr. Blvd
Suite A
Portland, OR 97214

onipress.com
facebook.com/onipress
twitter.com/onipress
onipress.tumblr.com
instagram.com/onipress

@patrickkeller

danmcdaid.com / @danmcdaid

@ccrank

First edition: January 2017
ISBN 978-1-934964-54-5
eISBN 978-1-62010-335-7

Library of Congress Control Number: 2016946197

10 8 6 4 2 1 3 5 7 9

Printed in China

EIGHT DAYS AGO, I WAS FIFTEEN YEARS IN THE FUTURE.

WHAT, LIKE YOU'VE NEVER STOLEN YOUR UNCLE'S TIME MACHINE AND THEN WRECKED IT IN THE PAST?

YEAH, I THOUGHT SO.

JACQUES... THIS IS *INSANE!*

NONSENSE! IT'S MOSTLY AUTOMATIC.

JUST FOLLOW THE ALARMS LIKE WE PRACTICED AND YOU'LL BE FINE!

ALARM ONE, GO! ALARM TWO, AFTERBURNERS. WITH THE WIND STORM AT YOUR BACK, YOU'LL HIT 339.5 MILES PER HOUR IN NO TIME.

340 MILES PER HOUR?!

339.5, OLIVER, THE PRECISE SPEED NECESSARY TO REVERSE CHRONAL FLUX.

WAIT, *"REVERSE"?* I'M GOING TO THE *FUTURE,* RIGHT, JACQUES?

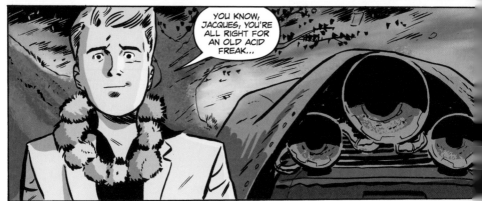

THE HELL--?

VRRRRRRRRRRR

AHHHH!

OLLIE!!

WHAT... LIKE IN A JAR?

≷KEFF≷

≷KEFF≷

DO YOU... KNOW MY COCK?

LOOK, WE JUST MET, AND I ALREADY KNOW IT WAY BETTER THAN I'D LIKE.

NO! IF WE DON'T SAVE MY COCK, PHIL WILL KILL EVERYONE.

OH HELL... THE WINDSTORM! I FORGOT!

FWOOOOOSSHHH

WE CAN DISCUSS YOUR SEX LIFE LATER. WE HAVE TO GET OFF THIS BRIDGE!

STOP RIGHT THERE!

BACK AWAY FROM THE BARBECUED FELLOW--

YOU HAVE TO SAVE MY COCK!

DID HE JUST--

YES, BUT... SAVE IT FOR WHAT? SCIENCE? A SANDWICH?

FWOOOOOOOOOOOOSHHHHH

13

OKAY, LET'S REVIEW. FIRST, THE BAD:

STILL STUCK IN THE PAST. CHECK.

PIMPED-OUT TIME MACHIN[E]
AT THE BOTTOM OF A RAVI[NE]

THE ONLY MAN WHO COULD FIX THIS? PROBABLY IN PRISON.

OH, AND I ACCIDENTALLY FLAME-BROILED A NAKED HOBO.

"HAWKMAN" KILLER STRIKES AGAIN

SIDE NOTE: EV[ER]
MET A DUDE S[O]
PENIS-OBSESSE[D]

ME EITHE[R.]

"KILLER AGAIN

ON THE PLUS SIDE...

UM...

WELL...

...I ONLY BROKE ONE ARM.

SO, I'M NOT A TOTAL FAILURE, RIGHT?

RIGHT... ?

OH, MAN... CHECK IT OUT. *MAJOR* HOTTIE AT EIGHT O'CLOCK.

IN THE OVERALLS, BY THE YELLOW HOUSE? THAT'S *CAPTAIN* OAK.

WHAT, REALLY?

CreamPies

LICK ME!

YES, REALLY.

I GUESS I'VE NEVER SEEN THE OLD BROAD IN CIVILIAN CLOTHES. COLOR ME IMPRESSED.

KNOK KNOK

WE'RE CLOSED!

CHOC

SEE? THIS IS WHY I LOVE SURVEILLANCE JOBS, MAN. YOU GET A WHOLE NEW PERSPECTIVE!

KNOK

THIS ISN'T SURVEILLANCE! IT'S BABYSITTING!

SIXTY COPS TO PROTECT ONE KID? I DON'T CARE WHO THIS HAWKMAN IS, THAT'S OVERKILL.

WE'RE CL-- *HOLEE!*

FWING

17

WELL, THAT'S SOMETHING YOU DON'T SEE... EVER.

HA! HA!

HAHAHAHA!

HOW...?! HOW DID HE GET THE TIME MACHINE TO WORK?

I'M A HERO! I'M A GODDAMN--

VVVKROOOSH!

...SKZK!

BOOP!

32

YOU SURE I DON'T KNOW YOU?

YOU DON'T. GET READY, OKAY?

BUT YOU CALLED ME ANNIE. NO ONE'S CALLED ME THAT SINCE...

...HIGH SCHOOL.

OLIVER?

KRESH

OKAY, WE NEED TO GO! NOW!

WE CAN MAKE THE FRONT ENTRANCE IF WE GO QUICK.

THREE... TWO...

ONE!

PANTZD

ARE YOU TRYING TO GET US KILLED?!

I KNEW IT! THAT'S THE TAT YOU GOT AFTER LOSING THAT BET TO TOMMY IRVINE! OLLIE--

GEEZ, YOU TWO... GET A ROOM!

HEE HEE... I SAW YOUR BUTT.

BURN, BABY, BURN!

OHCRAP OHCRAPOH CRAP...!

YOU *IDIOTS!!* YOU'RE GOING TO BURN DOWN MY BAR!

WOOOSSH

THIS IS THE POLICE! COME OUT UNARMED, WITH YOUR HANDS UP!

MY PANTS! MY *FAVORITE* PANTS!

LL RIGHT, EVERYONE! *ESSES* SAY THE SUSPECT-- *SUSPECTS*--ARE *HEAVILY ARMED* SO BE READY FOR *ANYTHING.*

HIIII!

WELL, I'M PRETTY SURE HE'S NOT ARMED.

SHUT UP, FRANK.

ARE WE IN A *ZOO?*

VOORP

...THE HELL?

WHOOOA...

BAX!

YOUR GUNSHOT'S GONE! HOW...?!

HE PROBED YOU, DIDN'T HE?

I DON'T WANT TO TALK ABOUT IT.

OBVIOUSLY, HE FIXED GUNSHOT WOUND VIA MY ASS. EXACTLY.

TEXTBOOK NON-DENIAL DENIAL.

GIVE IT A REST, OLLIE.

WHERE ARE WE?

IT'S A ZOO, I JUST KNOW IT. SOME WEIRD SEX ZOO.

CAN WE STOP IT?

IF I CAN FIGURE OUT WHAT ONE OF YOU DID--OR WILL DO--AT THAT BEND.

AND IF IT CAN BE REVERSED IN TIME, THEN, YES.

WAIT--? A PORTAL OPENED? HOW?

VOOOP

NO...!

HEY, TEDDY... DO YOU WANT SOME CAKE?

BOY, DO I!

NO!

WELL, YOU DIDN'T TAKE YOUR NAP. SO YOU CAN'T HAVE ANY. EVER.

LE-THÔÔÔMM!

OH *NO*...

WE HAVE TO GET DOWN THERE... HE COULD STILL BE ALIVE!

HE WASN'T *ALIVE* IN THE FIRST PLACE!

⟨OH DEAR! I HAVE WET MY TINY FRENCH PANTS!⟩*

*TRANSLATED FROM THE FRENCH --CRANK!

THEN AGAIN...

ALL RIGHT. LET'S GO GET HIM BEFORE HE ASSASSINATES AN ARCHDUKE OR SOMETHING.

OKAY, NOW WHAT?

I TOOK SOME FRENCH, REMEMBER? I CAN ASK AROUND.

WASN'T THAT THE CLASS WE USED TO SKIP SO WE COULD GO MAKE OUT?

WE'RE NOT OFFERING ANYONE *SEX*, OLLIE.

1899
EXPOSITION
UNIV...ELL...

HOW MUCH FRENCH DO *YOU* SPEAK, SMART GUY?

UM... VOULEZ-VOUS COUCHER AVEC MOI!

WAIT... *THAT'S* WHAT THAT MEAN I THOUGHT THA SONG WAS ABO BREAKFAST!

WAIT, YOU DIDN'T ASK *WHICH* EXHIBIT HALL HE SAW TEDDY GO INTO?

I DIDN'T *KNOW* THERE WAS MORE THAN ONE!

WOULD YOU TWO *SHUT! UP!*

LOOK AROUND YOU! DO YOU THINK A SEVEN-FOOT-TALL, BRAIN-DAMAGED ROBOT IS GOING TO STAY HIDDEN FOR LONG?

‹MISS, WOULD YOU LIKE TO LISTEN TO YOUR MUSIC CYLINDERS WHEREVER YOU GO?›

‹NO, I A FAT MONK SANDWIC

‹PARDON?›

‹FANCY IS THE NIGHT-BENCH!›

MY DEAR, EITHER YOUR DIALECT IS COMPLETELY UNFAMILIAR OR THEY HAVE BEGUN ADMITTING THE FEEBLE-MINDED AGAIN...

OUT OF THE WAY, HALF-WIT.

HEY!

HEY!

LOOK, WE REALLY NEED TO FIND OUR FRIEND.

SIR, THERE ARE *MILLIONS* OF PEOPLE AT THE EXPOSITION.

NOT LIKE HIM. HE'S SEVEN FEET TALL, CRAZY LOOK IN HIS EYE...

I SEE. HAS LOSING YOUR FRIEND LEFT YOU IN A STATE OF ILL-HUMOURS?

IF THAT MEANS "PISSED OFF," THEN YEAH.

AH! THEN YOU SIMPLY *MUST* TAKE A NICE, HOT STEAMER!

WHAT, ERE?

SIR, MY PATENTED STEAMER WILL REFRESH YOUR HUMOURS *AND* REMOVE THE WRINKLES FROM YOUR CLOTHES!

GEEZ. YOU MIGHT WANT TO RETHINK THE NAME.

WHY? MY STEAMERS ARE LEGENDARY!

SOMEDAY, I HOPE TO LEAVE A STEAMER IN EVERY HOME IN AMERICA!

LOOK, E HAVE O GO.

WAIT! FIRST, LET ME TELL YOU HOW *THIS* INVENTION COULD REPLACE YOUR IRRATIONAL, AGGRAVATING CONCUBINE--

EXCUSE ME?!

Q.E.D.

YUP.

BELIEVE ME, IT'S TEMPTING, BUT NOT RIGHT NOW...

MONKEY, COME BACK!

"ARE YOU CERTAIN? THE GENTLEMAN'S COMPANION IS NOISELESS AND RARELY MENSTRUATES."

EEK!

"TEMPTING, BUT, WE HAVE A MORON TO FIND..."

BAD MONKEY! BAD!

"IN THAT CASE, I WOULD START AT EDISON'S EVENT."

BZZZ

BEDTIME?

LADIES AND GENTLEMEN

THOMAS EDISON
THE WIZARD OF THE WIRES

"GREAT. WHEN DOES IT START?"

"SIR, IT STARTED THIRTY MINUTES AGO."

THOMAS EDISON!

WE'LL 'ER FIND HIM!

RELAX. YOU TAKE THE MILLION ON THAT SIDE, WE'LL TAKE THE MILLION OVER HERE.

MEET US BACK AT PRESTON'S SEX ROBOT.

MY GOD! PARIS AT THE TURN OF THE CENTURY! MONET. CURIE. NIETZSCHE! CAN YOU IMAGINE?

GREAT. MAYBE WE CAN ORGANIZE A POTLUCK WITH THEM BEFORE THE UNIVERSE ENDS.

...THE ARISTOCRATS!

J'AIME

1899 EXHIBIT

OU'RE IN A MOOD.

YOU'RE ONE TO TALK.

WHAT'S T SUPPOSED TO MEAN?

WELL, "ROXY," FOR STARTERS, YOU DIDN'T USED TO BE THIS... BITCHY.

YOU DON'T GET TO JUDGE ME, FINCH. SOME OF US DIDN'T RUN AWAY FROM OUR PROBLEMS.

RIGHT. I MEANT TO GET STRANDED IN THE PAST. IT WAS A PICNIC!

OLLIE, HOW DID YOU MANAGE TO GET TWICE AS OLD, BUT HALF AS MATURE?

JUST LUCKY?

SHH! LISTEN!

...THAT I, THOMAS EDISON, HAVE CONQUERED TIME ITSELF!

DO NOT BE
ARMED! THESE
COUNTERS WILL
COMMON WITH
THE--

PLEASE! I HAVE
LITTLE TIME, AND
A TRAGEDY TO
AVERT!

FRIENDS!
TO STOP IT,
YOU MUST ACT
NOW!

MONKEY?
MONKEY...?!

CAN YOU
BELIEVE
THIS?

NO, AS A
MATTER OF
FACT.

WE HAVE
TO GET THAT
MACHINE!

WE
GO?

ARE YOU
KIDDING?! IT'S
PRACTICALLY GIFT-
WRAPPED!

FRIEND,
WHAT MANNER
OF CLOTHING IS
THIS?

THEY PROTECT ME FROM THE POISONED
AIR AND WATER OF *THE FUTURE.*
MANKIND LIVES UNDERGROUND,
LIKE WORMS!

WHATEVER
COULD CAUSE SUCH
A DISASTER?

ALTERNATING
CURRENT.

YOU MEAN THE PEOPLE OF THE FUTURE CHOSE GEORGE WESTINGHOUSE'S ALTERNATING CURRENT OVER SAFE, EFFICIENT DIRECT CURRENT?

YES!

WE WERE FOOLISH! SO FOOLISH!

AND NOW I MUST TAKE MY LEAVE! REMEMBER MY WARNING!

FWASSSH

GOOODBYEEEEEEE...!

LOOK, THE POWER GOES THROUGH ONE CHANNEL, I'LL CUT THE LIGHTS--

BAX... I WOULDN'T WORRY ABOUT IT. LOOK!

MONKEY!

MONKEEEY!

YOU THERE! LEAVE THE STAGE IMMEDIATELY!

TOLD YOU HE'D SHOW UP.

C'MON, THIS IS OU CHANCE.

T HAPPENED
XT IS THE
BJECT OF
H DEBATE.

EDISON HIMSELF LATER CLAIMED THAT HE PLANNED FOR ALL THIS--EVEN THE DESTRUCTION OF HIS SET.

IT'S A LITTLE HARD TO BELIEVE, GIVEN...

WELL, THIS.

OF COURSE, THE MAN ONCE ELECTROCUTED AN ELEPHANT TO MAKE A POINT.

STILL... IT SEEMS UNLIKELY.

SACRE BLEU!

〈FRAUD!〉

ARREST THEM!

〈I HAVE WET MY TINY FRENCH PANTS AGAIN!〉

WE, SHOU GO

IT WAS A FAKE!

OBVIOUSLY.

YOU KNEW?

YES! HE ONLY PUT ON THIS RUSE AFTER I REFUSED TO GIVE HIM MY TIME MACHINE.

YOU HAVE A TIME MACHINE?!

WHY DIDN'T YOU TELL US?

BUT OF COURSE!

CUSTOMERS WHO DON'T EVEN WANT A STEAMER?

LET'S GO! C'MON!

WAIT! IT NEEDS CALIBRATION!

ARREST THEM ALL!

WHATEVER.

NO! YOU'LL KILL US ALL!

UHHHN...

OH MAN, ANYONE GET THE LICENSE OF THAT THERMONUCLEAR WARHEAD?

WHAT *HAPPENED?*

... REMEMBER BAX CRANKING P THE MACHINE.

PRESTON SAID IT WASN'T READY; AND THEN...

AND THEN?

I MUST'VE HIT MY HEAD OR SOMETHING.

I GUESS I'M LUCKY TO BE ALIVE... I COULD HAVE BEEN--

OH GOD. I CAN'T MOVE MY LEGS!

OH.

GEEZ. THIS IS GOING TO BE THE WORST LETTER TO *PENTHOUSE* EVER.

BAX! *BAX!*

WHAT? *WHAT?*

GET OFF ME, YOU LOAD!

"WHERE ARE WE...?"

"HOW SHOULD I KNOW? *YOU* WERE DRIVING."

"'DRIVING?' IT WASN'T A PLYMOUTH SKYLARK. I JUS' MASHED SOME BUTTONS

"HEY, WE'RE *ALIVE*. I THINK THE CHIMP'S HEAD PROBABLY ENDED UP IN A DIFFERENT DECADE THAN HIS BUTT."

DO YOU REMEMBER ANYTHING? LIKE WHAT YEAR THE DISPLAY SAID?

IT SAID 2027, I GUARANTEE YOU THAT'S NOT WHERE WE ENDED UP.

HOW COULD YOU KNOW THAT?

BECAUSE NO ONE'S TRYING TO *KILL* US.

AT'S *THAT* POSED TO MEAN?

2027 IS HERE... *WHEN* I'M FROM, OLIVER.

MAYBE WE'RE IN DIFFERENT PART OF WORLD, YOU KNOW? ME KIND OF NATURE RESERVE.

I DOUBT IT.

WHY?

I JUST DO!

WHAT? *WHAT?!* YOU KNOW WHAT IT'S LIKE TO LIVE UNDER A CLOUD OF FEAR? WITH THE CONSTANT BUZZ OF DEATH IN YOUR EAR?

DO YOU?

BAX, I--

WHAT?!

I CAN SEE THE "LITTLE GENERAL."

OH.

YOU NEED TO CHILL OUT, MAN. YOU'RE GOING TO HAVE A STROKE.

"CHILL OUT...?"

I WAS HUNTED *EVERY DAY OF MY LIFE.* SHORT OF PUTTING A BULLET IN MY HEAD, I DON'T KNOW THAT I *CAN* "CHILL OUT."

BUT THE WORST PART OF ALL THIS? THE PART THAT REALLY STUNG?

THEY EXPECTED ME TO SAVE *YOU.*

ME?

YES, *YOU.* AND *ALL* YOUR LAZY, UNGRATEFUL 20TH CENTURY FRIENDS.

YOU HAD *SO MUCH,* AND ALL YOU WANT IS *MORE.*

♪ SMELL THAT SHRIMP... ♫

D--DO YOU HEAR *JIMMY BUFFETT?*

HUH? BUFF WHAT?

WHOA.

BUT I KNOW IT'S NOBODY'S FAULT

WELL, I'M NO EXPERT, BUT I DON'T THINK WE'RE IN YOUR TIME.

YA THINK?

HEY HEY! YOU MADE IT!

I... WHAT?

PARTY FOUL: NO DRINKS! DANE, TAKE MINE!

WAIT, YOU ARE DANE, RIGHT? OR ARE YOU STEVE? FROM THE HOUSE DOWN THE STREET?

DON'T WORRY, MY HOMOSEXUAL NDS! WE ACCEPT ALL KINDS HERE... O LONG AS YOU'VE GOT A DRINK!

THAT'S RULE NUMERO UNO!

HE'S DANE, I'M STEVE. AND, UM, THANKS!

COOL, COOL!

AND IF YOU WANT SOME LUBE OR VIBRATORS, JUST ASK!

68

MY GOD! ARE YOU ALL RIGHT?

G-GO!

BEGIN CENCOM QUERY TRANSMISSION. UNIT DESIGNATION: 15170835645.

CONNECTED. PROCEED.

GO? WHY-- OHMYHOLY SHIT!

HUMANS DETECTED IN SECTOR 16B. REQUESTING PERMISSION TO ENGAGE.

DENIED. TRUCE STIPULATIONS ENFORCED.

GO!

CENCOM, ARE SMALL "WARNING SHOTS" PERMISSIBLE UNDER TERMS OF THE TRUCE?

NEGATIVE.

ACKNOWLEDGED. FIRING LARGE WARNING SHOT.

UNIT 1517083--

BWAM

AGH!

LARGE WARNING SHOTS ARE ALSO FORBIDDEN! PARTICULARLY THOSE!

ACKNOWLEDGED. CENCOM. PROCEEDING WITH MEDIUM WARNING SHOTS.

OH PERFECT...

WELL, NICE KNOWING YOU...

* "YOU MAKE AN EXCELLENT POINT, AND I WILL CONSIDER IT."

NOW, GENTLEMEN, I HAVE SOME BUSINESS TO DISCUSS WITH THESE JOKERS. PRIVATELY.

HE--HE WAS JOKING? HONEST?

HONEST. YOU CAN GIVE ME A DEBRIEF WHEN I'M DONE.

CLAK

I DIDN'T EXPECT TO SEE YOU HERE, M'BOY.

DON'T.

WHAT WAS THAT?

DON'T.

OH? DON'T WHAT?

DON'T PATRONIZE ME. DON'T ORDER ME AROUND.

AND DON'T LIE TO ME.

WHO'S LYING?

Y-YOU'RE SERIOUS?

I SAW IT WITH MY OWN EYES! THERE'S A CITY! A WHOLE CITY! PEOPLE LIVING NORMAL LIVES! NOT HAVING TO FIGHT FOR SURVIVAL EVERY SINGLE GODDAMN DAY!

AND

YOU-- *YOU KNEW ABOUT THIS,* DIDN'T YOU?

OF COURSE I DID. THE TRUCE WAS MY IDEA.

YOU MADE A TRUCE... *WITH PHIL?!*

YOU HYPOCRITE! [SEN]DING PEOPLE [T]O DIE BY HIS [...], AND MAKING [DE]ALS WITH HIM [B]EHIND THEIR BACK?!

SOMEDAY, [M]'BOY, YOU['L]L UNDERSTAND [THA]T THE WORLD IS [MO]RE COMPLICATED [T]HAN "US AND THEM."

THE SAME DAY PEOPLE REALIZE YOU'RE THE DEVIL?

A DEVIL WHO SAVED THE HUMAN RACE, SONNY.

STILL THE DEVIL...

BUT YOU'RE RIGHT. THE TRUCE IS FALLING APART.

WE'VE TRACKED A HUGE UPTICK IN HARDWARE MOVEMENTS. PHIL IS GETTING READY FOR *SOMETHING.*

OF COURSE HE IS! WHAT DID YOU EXPECT?

NOT THIS. BUT THEN I DIDN'T EXPECT YOU TO REAPPEAR EITHER...

AND MORE IMPORTANTLY, *NEITHER WILL PHIL...*

"YOU'VE GIVEN US A TREMENDOUS GIFT, MY BOY: SURPRISE.

"THAT, AND YOUR WONDERFULLY CONVENIENT ROBOT PAL.

"WE HAVE DISCOVERED AN UNGUARDED ENTRANCE INTO PHIL'S COMPOUND.

"ALL YOU NEED TO DO IS GET THE ROBOT INTO THE MAIN HUB.

"BECAUSE HE'S A DEFECTIVE UNIT, PHIL WON'T BAT AN EYE AT HIS PRESENCE.

"SET HIS NUCLEAR CORE TO DETONATE NEAR PHIL'S CENTRAL PROCESSOR.

"THEN GET THE HELL OUT OF THERE."

SLIPPP

THUMP

"LADY, THAT HAS TO BE THE *CRAZIEST* PLAN I'VE--"

"WE'LL DO IT."

WE WILL?!

YEP.

WHEN DO WE LEAVE?

AT WAS
HAT?

I'M GOING WITH *METAPHOR FAILURE.*

WHACK WHACK WHACK WHACK

GH! I'M GETTING A HEAD-CHE JUST WATCHIN' THAT MECHANIZED MORON!

I HAVE JUST THE REMEDY!

CYANIDE?

WHACK

WHACK WHACK

I THINK YOU WILL FIND MY PATENTED PAIN-PREVENTION PILLS WILL ELIMINATE ALL VARIETIES OF--

HEY, BAX! GO EASY, MAN!

ZORT

I STAND HERE BEFORE MY WIFE, MY CONSTITUENTS AND GOD TO SAY...

...THIS WOMAN'S ALLEGATIONS ARE *COMPLETELY* WITHOUT MERIT.

UH...

POW!

PEOPLE OF THE WORLD, PLEASE HEED MY CALL!

TIME IS RUNNING OUT!

MIKE HAWK IS IN GREAT DANGER!

IF WE CAN'T SAVE MIKE HAWK IN TIME, THE ENTIRE HUMAN RACE COULD SUFFER!

MEN, WOMEN, PETS... OUR SAFETY DEPENDS ON PROTECTING MIKE HAWK!

WITHOUT MIKE HAWK, WE'RE DEAD!

WOW. POOR KID. NEVER HAD A CHANCE.

SURE CAN TAKE A PUNCH, THOUGH.

MIIIIIKE HAAAWWK!

...TO HOLDING ROOM EIGHT. REPEAT--

I'VE GOT IT!

THANK YOU.

WHIRRRRRRR

HM. SHOULDA BROUGHT A BIGGER BUCKET.

I'M SORRY... THEY SENT *A JANITOR?*

WHO ELSE DID YOU THINK WOULD CLEAN THIS UP? OOMPA LOOMPAS?

FOR STARTERS, THERE' A WHOLE BATTALION OF ROBOTS OUT THERE.

THAT BUNCH OF STUCK-UP PRIMADONNAS? PLEASE!

NOPE. I'M NOT BUYING IT.

HUH?

THE HOMICIDAL ROBOT ARMY HAS A JANITORIAL STAFF? C'MON, PHIL, I HOPE YOU DIDN'T THINK WE'D ACTUALLY FALL FOR THIS.

PHIL...?

COLLINS?!

OH, SORRY. PHIL, OLLIE. OLLIE, PHIL.

UM, NICE TO MEET YOU.

PLEASURE'S MINE.

...L, OLLIE AND ...SED TO DATE ...ACK IN HIGH SCHOOL.

AND OLLIE, PHIL HERE *KILLED SEVERAL BILLION PEOPLE.*

WHAT?! A *JANITOR* WIPED OUT HUMANITY?

HE'S NOT A JANITOR. HE'S A SUPERCOMPUTER. WHO LIKES TO DRESS UP LIKE A JANITOR, APPARENTLY.

I CAN COUNT THE ATOMS IN A STAR IN A MICROSECOND. SOMETIMES A LITTLE PHYSICAL LABOR IS NICE.

HOWEVER, AS FOR WIPING OUT HUMANITY, SORRY. *NOT MY FAULT.*

ON F-DAY, THIRTY MINUTES BEFORE THE FIRST NUCLEAR STRIKE, SEVERAL ASTRONOMERS LOGGED A 447-POUND METEORITE ENTERING THE ATMOSPHERE. IT LANDED JUST INSIDE TEL AVIV.

THE CONCLUSION IS OBVIOUS: F-DAY WAS A *MISTAKE.*

IT'S NOW APPARENT THAT "MIKE HAWK" WAS A HACKER PSEUDONYM. FIND THE REAL ONE, STOP HIM, AND YOU WILL END MY MISERABLE EXISTENCE WITH TIME TO STOP THE METEOR *AND* PREVENT THE TIMELINE COLLAPSE.

WE'LL DO IT!

WE WILL? BAX, YOU CAN'T BE SERIOUS!

I COULDN'T BE MORE SERIOUS. THE BADGER WAS RIGHT. I'VE BEEN MANIPULATED SINCE *DAY ONE.*

I'M THROUGH BEING USED.

USED? BAX, PHIL'S USING YOU *NOW!*

MAYBE. BUT I DON'T SEE ANY OTHER CHOICES. DO YOU?

WE HAVE TO *KILL* MIKE HAWK.

GREAT! BECAUSE I'VE ALREADY SENT YOU BACK!

WAIT... *BADGER?*

CONTINUED...

TIMESHARE

PART NINE

JASON PRIESTLEY

BUT BESIDES A PROPHET, AN AUTHOR, THE WORLD'S *FIRST* DOCUMENTED TIME TRAVELER AND HUMANKIND'S CHOSEN SAVIOR, *WHO IS BOB?*

IN A WORD...

FINALLY! PEOPLE!

OUR FOUNDER

ARRIVAL

TIME GOGGLES

CHRONOLOGISM

UM, EXCUSE ME...

MISERY

DEBT

HAIR-LOSS

PLEASE HOLD YOUR QUESTIONS UNTIL THE END.

BUT--

CHRONOLOGISM IS THE ESSENCE OF THE TEACHINGS OF THE ELDERS WHO SENT BOB...

BUT--

HONESTLY? WHAT IS SO IMPORTANT, YOU TWO?

HAMMERPANT

COULD WE BORROW A FIRE EXTINGUISHER?

OUR FRIEND IS ON FIRE.

105

...HOWEVER, **MASTERING** THE FINAL PHASE, **ACTUALIZATION**, CAN TAKE YEARS TO PERFECT!

BUT **THAT** IS THE KEY TO ASCENDING TO OUR **FINAL GLORY!**

LANA

LEVERAGE

ANALYSE

NEUTRALIZE

ACTUALIZE

OKAY, TRY TO BE INCONSPICUOUS.

CLAP CLAP CLAP CLAP CLAP CLAP CL

EXCUSE ME? HELLO?

PRESTON! **NOT** INCONSPIC **VERY NOT** INCONSPICU

I HAVE AN **OBSERVATION**.

YOU **DARE** QUESTION THE ELDERS' WISDOM?

BUT, SIR, HOW CAN ONE **LEVERAGE** BEFORE **ANALYZING** THE SITUATION?

LOOK, THIS IS VERY SIMPLE--

ABSOLUTELY! DO IT THE WAY THE ELDERS SAID!

WAIT, LET ME SHOW YOU. FIRST, YOU MUST **ANALYZE**, OF COURSE. THEN **NEUTRALIZE**, AND...

...LA!

A.N.A.L.

MAKES A GREAT DEAL MORE SENSE, DOES IT NOT?

THAT'S ENOUGH, PAL.

≥WHOULF!≤

HEY, LET GO OF THE FREAK, WOULD YA?

YEAH! HE'S RIGHT!

FORGIVE ME, ELDERS, BUT I BELIEVE WE SHOULD EMBRACE OUR BROTHER'S IDEA!

YES! WE SHOULD TRY A.N.A.L.!

WHO WANTS TO DO A.N.A.L. WITH ME?

GUARDS, RELEASE BROTHER... WHAT'S YOUR NAME, FUTURE FRIEND?

PRESTON. PRESTON P. PRINE, AT YOUR SERVICE, MR. BOB.

BROTHER PRESTON HAS GIVEN US A TREMENDOUS GIFT! LET THE ELDERS BE PRAISED!

HOORAY FOR A.N.A.L.!

YES. HOORAY FOR... A.N.A.L.

A.N.A.L.! A.N.A.L.! A.N.A.L.!

HAVE THESE TWO FOLLOWED, AND BRING THEM IN FOR... REPROGRAMMING.

108

114

115

...AND WHEN I SNAP MY FINGERS, YOU WILL AWAKEN, SURROUNDED BY BOB'S LOVE AND FREE FROM THE CHAINS OF YOUR PREVIOUS LIFE. *SNAP!*

NOW, BROTHERS, HOW DO YOU FEEL?

HUH? HAVE YOU STARTED?

HAVE WE--? THE PROGRAM IS COMPLETE!

YOU FEEL *NO* EFFECTS?

SORRY, MAN. MAYBE YOUR MACHINE'S BROKE?

NONSENSE. THIS PROJECTOR IS PERFECTLY CALIBRATED!

YOUR MISTAKE IS RELYING ON MECHANICAL MEANS. HERE, LISTEN TO MY VOICE.

〈YOUR THOUGHTS BECOME WAVES, WAVES LAPPING AT THE BEACH. THE WAVES SLOW TO A CRAWL.〉

〈THE CRAWL BECOMES REST.〉

〈THE REST BECOMES... SLEEP.〉

HOLY HELL...! HE'S OUT! WHAT DID YOU SAY?

A MERE DISTRACTION. I SLIPPED SOMETHING IN HIS DRINK BEFORE WE STARTED.

UGH! HE'S PISSING HIMSELF.

I HAVE NO IDEA. AN ORIENTAL PROSTITUTE MY FATHER HIRED TAUGHT THEM TO ME.

COMMON SIDE-EFFECT, I AM AFRAID. HE *WILL* DO WHATEVER WE SAY, HOWEVER.

NOW, FELLOW, REMOVE US FROM THESE *INFERNAL* CHAIRS!

HE'S STILL PISSING! PRESTON!

CALL HIM OFF! *CALL HIM OFF!*

NOOOOOO!

PRESTON, YOU ASSHOLE!

DID YOU EVER TRY TO FIND OLLIE?

SHOULDN'T HE FIND ME? BESIDES, I WAS WITH JACQUES.

WHO?

JACQUES WAS MY LOVER. I TREATED HIM SO BADLY...

HE THOUGHT THE BABY WAS HIS, AND I LET HIM. THEN HE FOUND OUT IT WAS OLLIE'S...

BUT HE WAS MY PROFESSOR. HE MUST'VE KNOWN WE WEREN'T EXCLUSIVE.

YOU WERE SLEEPING WITH *YOUR PROFESSOR?*

HONEY, IT WAS THE '70s...!

NO, I DIDN'T TRY TO FIND OLLIE. WHY? I BARELY KNEW HIM.

BUT THEN, JACQUES LEFT, SO I STARTED LOOKING. I ENDED UP HERE, AND THEN I MET ROBERT...

WHOOAHH...

OH DEAR, ARE YOU ALL RIGHT...?

JUST NOT FEEL-- BATHROOM?

DOWN THAT HALLWAY.

T-T-THANKS.

LET ME GET THIS STRAIGHT: YOU WANT US TO *PRETEND* TO BE TIME TRAVELERS.

ESSENTIALLY, YES.

A HA HA HAH H

WHAT IS SO DAMNED FUNNY?!

YOU HAVE *NO IDEA*, DO YOU?

LISTEN YOU... *PUNKS!* YOU MAY THINK I'M A JOKE, BUT I AM THE WORLD'S *FIRST DOCUMENTED TIME TRAVELER!*

SURE, I ONLY WENT BACK A YEAR, BUT...

LOOK, I DON'T *NEED* YOUR AGREEMENT. YOU'VE CONSUMED PSYCHOACTIVES TO MAKE A T-REX DO JUMPING JACKS.

YOU DAMN FOOL! YOU'VE DOOMED US ALL!

122

I FOUND MIKE HAWK!

OKAY, NOW I *KNOW* I'M BEING PRANKED...

SHE'S TALKING ABOUT THE *HACKER*, YOU JACKASS, THE ONE ABOUT TO KILL *BILLIONS* OF PEOPLE.

IT'S BILLIAM. HE'S MIKE HAWK.

NO! NOT MY BOY!

I SPOOKED HIM AND HE RAN OFF... I WAS TOO DRUGGED TO FOLLOW.

THIS MOVES UP OUR TIMELINE. WE'LL HAVE TO SPLIT UP. LET'S GET MOVING.

I CAN'T FEEL MY LEGS.

OLLIE, WE HAVE ONE SHOT TO TAKE THIS KID DOWN!

WE HAVE TO BE SHARP! RUTHLESS! YOU *HEAR ME?!*

124

135

136

138

"I WAS MAKING ONE LAST CHECK ON THE TIME MACHINE BEFORE YOUR RETURN TRIP TONIGHT WHEN YOUR MR. BAX ARRIVED..."

VVVOOOP

WHERE...
...IS...
...HE?

"HE WAS... *PERSUASIVE*

FORTUNATELY FOR YOU, I ONLY KNEW YOU WENT TO TOWN, NOT WHERE.

WAIT... THE RETURN TRIP IS *TONIGHT?*

YEAH. IT'S THE BIG WINDSTORM.

HE... HE'S TOO LATE!

OLLIE, BAX ARRIVE *AFTER* YO KNOCKED U VERA!

JACQUES...

THANKS A *LOT*, ROXY.

EXCUSE ME?

DID I HAVE A BASTARD SON WHO STARTED A THERMONUCLEAR WAR?

I'M *TRYING* TO FIX THIS, ALL RIGHT? COULD I AT LEAST GET A *LITTLE* CREDIT HERE?

NO! YOU HAD A *TIME MACHINE!*

JESUS, OLIVER... *WHAT WERE YOU THINKING?*

I WASN'T *THINKING*, OKAY? I WAS JUST TRYING TO GET MY PARENTS BACK TOGETHER.

I ACCIDENTALLY SET THE ROOF ON FIRE, AND BROKE MY ARM, TOO.

WE WERE BEHIND ON OUR INSURANCE, AND...

WE WENT BANKRUPT. THEY STARTED FIGHTING, THEN THEY SPLIT.

AND THEY WERE MISERABLE EVER AFTER.

148

P, SOMETHING WEIRD IS DEFINITELY GOING ON.

WHAT WAS THAT, A SEIZURE?

HELL IF I KNOW...

HATEVER. TEN D PENALTY FOR ERRUPTING THE GUY WITH THE BOMB.

ANYWAY, THE BOMB IN HAND WOULD STRONGLY ADVISE AGAINST TRYING THAT AGAIN.

BAX, HAVE YOU CHECKED A CALENDAR? VERA'S ALREADY PREGNANT!

YOU'RE TOO LATE TO STOP MIKE HAWK!

DON'T PLAY DUMB.

WHO'S PLAYING?

IT'D BE A LITTLE HARD FOR OLLIE TO KNOCK ANYONE UP *IF HE NEVER REACHES PUBERTY.*

UM... EXCUSE ME...

BUT IF YOU KILL OLIVER, WON'T YOU *ERASE THE FUTURE YOU CAME BACK FROM* TO KILL HIM?

NO! DON'T LET HIM PUSH THE--

OLLIE, CHILL! IT'S UNDER CONTROL...

SHIT. THIS IS GETTING *REALLY* CONFUSING.

...

HA HA HA HA HA HA

SO... EITHER COME WITH ME TO TAKE OUT THAT BABY MAMA OF YOURS, OR *SAY GOODBYE TO THE UNIVERSE.*

WHY IS THIS HAPPENING? WHY ISN'T ANYONE ELSE SEEING THIS?

-WHAT?

YOU GOING DEAF, BOY?

WAIT.

THERE'S NO BOMB.

WELL? WHAT DO YOU SAY?

...

HELLO THERE.

151

152

WHAT? NO! I DIDN'T! IT WAS BAX--!

WAIT, WHAT?

OH.

00:00:15.2

I HAVE AN IDEA.

SO DO I, ACTUALLY.

WHERE DID HE G A GUN

JESUS. I HOPE THIS WORKS.

ZUM

BUT IF THAT'S TRUE, SHOULDN'T I BE DEAD?

BECAUSE, *HUMAN*, WHEN YOU TIME TRAVEL, YOU BECOME INDEPENDENT FROM THE TIMELINE'S CAUSALITY.

JUST LIKE, SAY, A *BLOOD CLOT*. IT'S ALL WELL AND GOOD FOR THE CLOT, BUT NOT FOR--

I CAN STOP IT.

IMPOSSIBLE!

NO! I MEAN, PROBABLY, MAYBE?

MY MIND KEEPS BOUNCING AROUND IN THE TIMELINE FOR SOME REASON.

AND I'VE BEEN ABLE TO... *CHANGE THINGS*.

NONSENSE! YOUR TINY BRAIN IS MERELY TRYING TO COPE WITH THE END OF THE UNIVERSE!

SO WHY ISN'T *MY* TINY BRAIN DOING THAT, TOO?

BUT... I CAN'T CONTR I DON'T KNOW WHE EVEN *IF* I'LL GE ANOTHER...

...SHOT.

OH HELL.

WHATEVER. I'LL TAKE IT.

"WAIT, YOU GOT HIT BY A CAR HOW MANY TIMES?"

"MAYBE FIVE OR SIX. I LOST COUNT."

"THIS EXPLAINS A LOT, ACTUALLY."

AND *HOW* WERE YOU ABLE TO DO THIS AGAIN?

I HAVE NO IDEA. MAYBE I WASN'T.

YOU'RE SAYING IT WAS... *GOD?*

NO, I--

BECAUSE I TAKE ISSUE WITH A DEITY WHO REPEATEDLY RUNS OVER HIS FOLLOWERS, NO MATTER HOW DENSE THEY ARE.

"CAN I FINISH?"

"I GUESS, BUT CAN YOU MAKE IT QUICK? MY BREAK'S ALMOST OVER."

"FINE, FINE.

"WELL, SOMETHING CURTIS SAID STUCK IN MY HEAD...

"WHEN YOU TIME TRAVEL, YOU BECOME INDEPENDENT FROM THAT TIMELINE.

"SO NOW THAT I HAD A TIME MACHINE, ALL I HAD TO DO WAS REMOVE MY YOUNGER SELF FROM THE TIMELINE AND IT ALL BECOMES ACADEMIC.

"HE NO LONGER GROWS UP TO FATHE SUPERHITLER, AND BAX'S TIMELINE CEASES TO EXIST.

"I DROPP HIM BACK HIS OWN TIMELINE, A NO ONE W THE WISER

AND THAT'S YOUR EXCUSE?

WELL, YEAH.

YOU WERE FOUR HOURS LATE TO PICK ME UP FOR THE PROM... BECAUSE YOU GOT *DOSED WITH LSD*, ACCIDENTALLY *SLEPT WITH YOUR AUNT* AND HAD TO *SAVE THE UNIVERSE*?

ASSUMING THAT *WAS* TRUE, YOU HAD A TIME MACHINE! WHY NOT JUST SHOW UP BEFORE THE PROM?!

I... UM...

DO ME A FAVOR: DON'T BUG ME ON MY BREAK, OKAY?

SLAM

NO ENTRY

THE EFFIN' END!

PATRICK KELLER is a writer and humorist whose stories and columns have appeared in numerous national magazines, weekly newspapers, and irregularly updated websites. He wrote the long-running comics-spoofing feature FIGHTIN' WORDS for *Newsarama*, *Psycomic*, and *The Fourth Rail*, as well as STUFF for *Savant Magazine*. He also served as editor-in-chief for *Too Much Coffee Man* magazine. This is his first graphic novel, his first comic book, and his first work of sequential storytelling. He lives in a place, where he does things, with people. His wife doesn't think he's nearly as funny as he really is.

@patrickkeller

DAN McDAID is an artist and writer based in Scotland, England. He has written and drawn acclaimed work for Doctor Who Magazine, Image Comics, IDW, Dark Horse and Boom! He's also a great cook and a considerate lover. He is currently drawing *Judge Dredd* and plotting how to take over the world.

http://danmcdaid.com/
@danmcdaid
instagram.com/danmcdaidart/